ADELAIDE'S TRUST

G. BAILEY

CONTENTS

MORE BOOKS BY G. BAILEY

HER GUARDIANS SERIES

HER FATE SERIES

PROTECTED BY DRAGONS SERIES

LOST TIME ACADEMY SERIES

THE DEMON ACADEMY SERIES

DARK ANGEL ACADEMY SERIES

SHADOWBORN ACADEMY SERIES

DARK FAE PARANORMAL PRISON SERIES

SAVED BY PIRATES SERIES

THE MARKED SERIES

HOLLY OAK ACADEMY SERIES

THE ALPHA BROTHERS SERIES

A DEMON'S FALL SERIES

THE FAMILIAR EMPIRE SERIES

FROM THE STARS SERIES

THE FOREST PACK SERIES

THE SECRET GODS PRISON SERIES

THE REJECTED MATE SERIES

FALL MOUNTAIN SHIFTERS SERIES

ROYAL REAPERS ACADEMY SERIES

THE EVERLASTING CURSE SERIES

THE MOON ALPHA SERIES

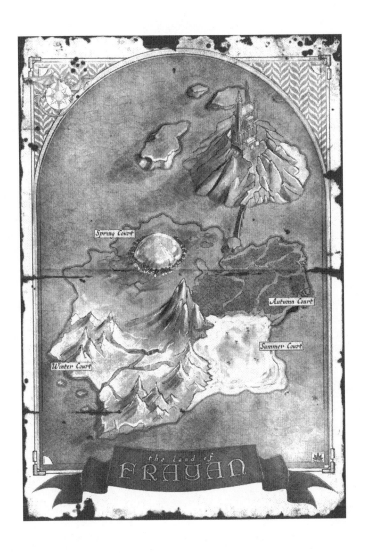

Spring Court

Autumn Court

Summer Court

Winter Court

the Land of FRAYAN

For all those who have read a book on a stormy night
and never wanted the storm to end.

DESCRIPTION

Does fate ever give you a choice?

When Adelaide moved to a sleepy little town in Scotland with her sister, the last thing she expected was to find out she isn't even from this world.
Now the world she was born in is at war, and they need a ruler.
They need a queen, just not the one who is currently ruling Fray.
Not the queen who will do anything to kill Adelaide and the men she has fallen for.
Rick, Nath, Mich and Josh have to keep Adelaide alive in a world none of them know or understand.

Or there will be nothing left once the prophesied war is over.

Her pack must save her.
Her fate must protect her.

The fates are close, and when they call, you don't have a choice.
Not when you are a wolf of fate...

PROLOGUE

"When the snow stops falling on the
    Winter court,
When the sun stops shining high
    above the Summer court,
When no creatures are born in the
    lands of the Spring court,
A storm will arise and destroy
    them all.
The Autumn court heir will return,
    bringing death as her shadow.
The Autumn court will rule, the
    Autumn court will prevail.
And all who are against her will fall.
On a stormy night, a queen will be
    born to the Summer court.

*Death will be her tool. Life will be her
ruin.
The heir of Summer and Autumn are
forever linked
by far more than their births alone.
For one cannot live without the other
dying at their hand.
There can only be one queen of the
Frayan courts..."*

"Father...is the heir of Summer me?" I ask my father as my mother holds his hand tightly, a rare show of affection and love. I'm sure it comes more from their fear of my actions, and less their love for each other. I've learnt that love is simply a tool to use against those closest to you. My parents promised me I would learn the truth on my sixteenth birthday, but I expected it would label me as queen, not give me an enemy that isn't even born yet. I have always wanted to know why they look at me in fear, and at other times they show me only disinterest. I am not a monster like they think...but I will not let this heir of the Autumn court take what is mine. I am the only queen of the Frayan courts, and I have known it since I was a child. I've read many books about the old ways of the fates, and I believe there should only be one leader of all of Frayan. Earth has a queen, and Dragca has its royal family. Why should Frayan be ruled by four courts and have four royal families when it could have just one?

"You were always a cold, cruel child. We hoped with age you would become kinder, see that death and misery are not the way to rule the court. Summer is a kind court, full of sweet Summer children. They need a queen who will put them first, not start a war due to a prophecy," my mother tells me, standing up as she speaks. "They will never love and trust you if you destroy them." She smooths down her light blue dress as she speaks; the dress is the very colour of the Summer court. It mimics the beautiful blue seas and blue skies. I have always loved my court, at least the beauty of it. The sun shines through the window, catching the many jewels on her large necklace, which is too big for her small neck. It's an odd thing to notice, but I have so hated them for so long. They reflect light into her strawberry blonde hair that falls around her shoulders much like my own hair does. She is beautiful but so very cold and never admits to such ways.

In public, she is all smiles and kind to everyone. Her home life is extremely different. It's no wonder I am such a cold, cruel child with a mother like her to learn from. My father, he is different, but he is so afraid of my mother that he would never defend me. Women in the royal Frayan lines always have the most power. Their wings, so red and bright, flutter behind them, as they both often forget to shut off their powers, the very blessing from the fates and old gods who abandoned us for better worlds. It's just a nasty reminder of the true reason they hate me so. I was born without wings, a blight to the royals who have always been blessed with wings. It's the only special thing about the royals, and I didn't get it. I don't know why the fates and old gods hate me so, but they will soon fear me at least. If I cannot fly, I will find another way to take what is mine.

"I will rule everyone, and no one will ever stop me. I will kill this Autumn court heir and make sure she can never take my power," I bitterly say.

"She will be the end of you, Lilyanne Summer. There will only be one queen of Frayan, and it will never be you."

MY MOTHER IS WRONG. It will be me, and I will never stop until I am queen of them all.

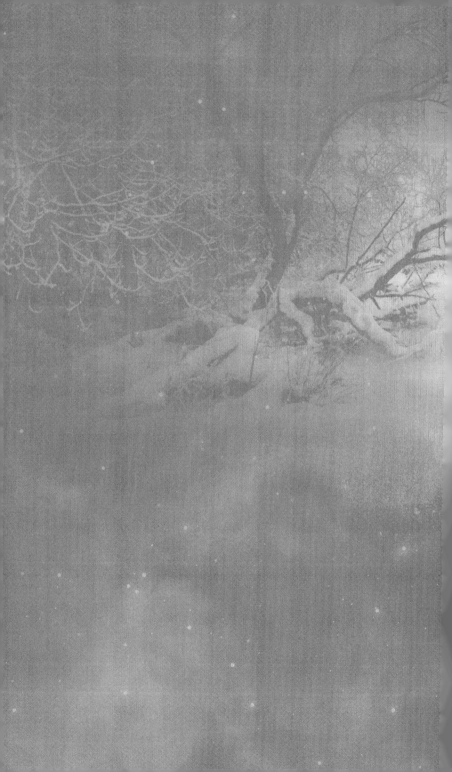

CHAPTER
ONE

ADELAIDE

All I can hear for a long time is an unusual buzzing noise, and it is so loud it stings against my ears. My body feels like it is on fire, like my soul itself is burning its way out of my body, and I am powerless to stop it. I've never felt magic like this, and it's terrible. *So terrible.* My stomach, arms and back feel like someone is drawing on them with a hot poker. I can't stop it. I can't move. The sides of my neck start to burn too, and the buzzing noise just seems to be getting louder until it hurts my ears more than the burning does. Finally, the scream I've been trying to make come out blasts out of my mouth, echoing in my ears so loudly it pushes away the buzzing.

A hand squeezes mine tightly, and the firm

hand somehow makes me feel a little better as I try to remember who it is. I can't even remember who I am through the pain. I focus on the hand in mine as I finally come to, looking up at the bright blue sky above me that is so very different from anything I've ever seen before. There are several clouds in the sky, one fully blocking the sun, yet it is so bright out here.

"Adie!" Josh's urgent voice calls to me just as all the sounds I was blocking out come rushing to my ears. The wind blowing through the trees, the sound of a bird squawking in the distance, and someone's heavy breathing. The smell of flowers and something sweet floats to me just as I scent that Josh is right by me. My wolf pushes against my mind, a low growl escaping my lips, and it hurts my sore throat from all the screaming. I turn my head to the side to see Josh kneeling there, his wavy black hair pushed out of his dark eyes that hold more than concern for me in them. His hand is holding mine, and his other hand moves to rest on my cheek, which is oddly sweet for Josh. Maybe he hit his head or something? "We need to get moving. This place can't be safe; it's too open."

"What are you talking about?" I groan as Josh helps me sit up, and I scratch my neck, where it still hurts from the burning, only to feel smooth skin and grumble because everything really hurts, but I don't seem to have any injuries. It takes me a few seconds to remember everything as I push aside the weird pain I'm currently in. I remember the handshake with Winter that opened some kind of portal and how horrified she looked. Josh and I went through the portal—oh, and I think Tay got pulled in with me, if I remember right.

"Adie, are you—"

"Where is Tay?" I ask Josh, interrupting whatever he was going to say as I stare around at the yellow grass we are sitting on as everything else comes back. I killed him. I killed Mr. Graves, and I know a part of me should feel guilty for taking a life...but I don't. He was a monster, one I am happy is gone. My mother, Asteria, died after years of torture, and she gave me my powers, which I don't understand. I swallow the emotion, not wanting to lose control like I did when she died. I can't do that here, not when I don't have a clue if we are in danger. The power I now have is like nothing else in the world I've ever experienced, and I don't want to tap into that again. Josh gives me one more concerned look, clearly wishing he could read my mind, before he stands up. He keeps looking around for Tay as he helps me stand up with him, though I'm a little shaky on my feet.

"There!" I point, seeing a little pink in the grass not far from us, as it moves a little. Josh runs over and picks her up, carrying her back to me in his arms. I may not be the pixie's biggest fan, but I don't want to see her hurt. Plus, my pack seems to like her. God, when did I start calling them *my* anything? I mean, they might hate me as I did go a little crazy with power at the end there.

"She must have hit her head coming through the portal. Maybe this is Dragca. I never went to visit it, but—" Josh starts saying, but I know he is wrong. I feel he is wrong, and I don't know how to explain it.

"It's Frayan, where I was born. I know it," I tell Josh, who stares at me in silence. I haven't told him a single thing about who I am, and I reckon it's going to bite me in the ass now.

"Seems you've been keeping some secrets, sweetheart," he replies, not looking impressed, but he is hardly one to talk about secrets. Since we met, he has done nothing but keep a million secrets from me, and I'm not one bit closer to guessing what they all are. I remember one thing though, that Queen Winter and her kings looked more scared of Josh than they did anyone else. I want to understand why, because Josh might be a bit of an arsehole, but there is something good about him as well.

"I'm not the only one. What exactly are you, Josh?" I retort, and he narrows his eyes at me like I'm the bad guy. Before either of us can carry on this argument, I hear footsteps crunching through the grass behind us, and my wolf quickly goes on guard. We both turn around, and I see Josh tuck Tay into his leather jacket, doing it up quickly as we watch a woman walk across the field.

She has a black cloak on, which sweeps across the grass behind her. Her dress is also black, but it is cut so it shows her stomach and chest off, with only a band of material across her breasts. The dress flows out into a long gown from her waist down, brushing against the grass as she walks. I meet her yellow eyes, which are similar to the eyes of an old cat that lived across the street in one of my many homes growing up. *Though I doubt telling her that would be a smart idea.* Her hair is strawberry blonde, cut short to her chin, and the top is braided to hold in the black crown.

The black crown is made of black crystals, all of them looking deadly sharp and reflecting the light. Everything about her is imposing, but I can't help thinking she is trying too hard. When I met Queen Winter, she was imposing, but it was more in a way that made you know she was important. She didn't have to wear all black and narrow her eyes in the tense way this woman does. She wants you to fear her, I'm sure of it. I wouldn't be surprised if she thinks she is the most important woman in the world. In all the worlds, now I think about it.

"Adelaide Autumn, heir to the Autumn court. How I have longed to finally meet you," the woman states, stopping not far in front of me. Her voice is nearly as sweet as her smile directed at me, but something makes me instantly not trust her. My wolf practically growls in my mind as I watch the woman with caution. "Oh, how rude of me. You do not know who I am, do you?"

"As I've never been to Frayan—"

"Tut, tut. Lies are not the Fray way. You know you've been here, as you were born on Frayan," she is quick to interrupt me before letting out a little laugh like it was funny to be rude. Her eyes flicker to my bracelet, the one that was my father's, and I watch how she seems shocked for a tiny second.

"Shame I wasn't here for more than a short

time as a baby and didn't learn the customs. How do you know who I am?" I ask her, and I'm curter than I wanted to be. I just don't like her, and I always trust my instincts. Natural instincts are a warning. It's the only way your soul can tell you something is wrong.

"I'm Queen Lilyanne of the Frayan courts," she tells me. I was right; she is important and clearly very up herself. Her name brings back a flash of memories from the books I read. The ones my mum left for me.

"I know about you and the prophecy! I read that you killed your parents and started a war. I —" I stop talking when I remember what she just said. I'm the heir to the Autumn court, and that prophecy talked about me as well. She was the one that killed my father and nearly my mother. Lilyanne is the reason I was sent to Earth, and my mother was captured there. All because of some prophecy that I don't even know the words of. The book didn't tell me it, and I have a feeling I need to know it to win anything against this woman.

"I killed your parents too, and I just missed out on you," she confirms what I already thought. I step back in shock, chancing a look towards Josh as he moves closer to me. I don't know why I'm

13

seeking him out for comfort, but right now, I need him more than I want to admit.

"You didn't kill Asteria," I counter with tears in my eyes. For a second, Lilyanne's resolve crumbles, and her eyes burn with anger and a touch of shock.

"Then you received your powers?" she bitterly asks, and I don't respond to her. We both know the answer as she runs her eyes over me and grits her teeth. "Well, that is a shame. I had planned to let you live and keep you as a reminder that I, Queen Lily, can be kind like the court I was born in. Death it will be, then, but first I want you to give me your powers."

"I don't think so," Josh interjects, his wings slamming out of his back as he protectively comes to my side. I run my eyes over his soft black wings, and my fingers itch to reach out and touch them.

"Demon child, your powers are so very useless here. What else can a half angel do but fly?" Lilyanne asks with a cruel chuckle. In a matter of seconds, she slams a beam of what I think is sunlight out of her hand, and it hits Josh in the chest before he can defend himself. He goes flying backwards as my heart catches in my chest.

"Josh!" I scream, watching his back hit a tree

so hard the bark cracks and snaps. He slides to the ground, but I can't see if he is okay from where I am. I turn back to Lilyanne as I shake with anger. I scream as lightning bursts out my hands, crackling all the way up my arms, and I gasp as I feel something on my back. I turn back for only a moment, seeing large blue wings that glitter and shimmer as they float on my back. *I have wings?!* I turn back to Lilyanne, who is now glowing bright, almost like the sun if it was full of glitter. Every part of her skin is glowing like the sun itself, and I lift my hands.

"Let us go, it doesn't have to be this way. I don't want to kill you," I tell her, because my parents taught me to try the peaceful option first. I'm pretty sure she is so crazy that my words are nothing but a joke to her. I could try being honest next. "I only want to go home with Josh."

"That is the problem. This is your home, Adelaide Autumn," Lilyanne responds with a cruel tilt of her lips as she lifts her hands. Before she can do anything else, a loud roar makes her look back just as a dragon swoops down out of the clouds. *Holy shit.* The dragon is blue-scaled, the scales shining in the sunlight as it roars, and it is massive. It lands right behind Lilyanne, who seems as shocked as I am. *Dragons are real?* In a matter of moments, the dragon breathes out a stream of cold ice, freezing Lilyanne in her place like a giant ice pop.

I step back as it spreads its wings and starts running towards me, its large paws making the whole ground shake. Shit, getting eaten by a dragon cannot be a good way to die. I turn around and start to run away, only for the dragon to catch me in its claws not long after and shoot us up into the sky. I scream as I see Josh on the ground, spreading his wings out and flying up to us. He uses his wings to glide next to us, and he reaches a hand out for me. I can't hear the words he says, but I think he is telling me it's going to be okay.

One thing is for sure, Josh is no Prince Charming who is here to save me. Turns out I get a dragon instead.

CHAPTER

TWO

ADELAIDE

The dragon almost gently drops me on the forest floor after a long flight, and I have to roll a few times to stop myself before pushing some of the fallen leaves in my mouth away. I pick myself up off the floor, brushing the rest of the dirt and leaves off me as I see Josh landing a little away from us. It had soon become clear Josh wasn't concerned about the dragon as he flew next to us, looking over the mountain we flew around until we got to this massive forest. I didn't look around too much, mainly because flying this high is not what I consider as fun.

The dragon disappears into a haze of white smoke before there is a man standing where the dragon once was. A very naked, extremely attractive guy. The guy smirks as he looks at me. His blue eyes are so crystal clear as we watch each other. I only have a second to take in how his blond hair is nearly white, shaved on the sides and thick in the middle. It falls into his forehead, almost in a playful way. I guess it isn't a big shock that there are dragon shifters out in the world. I mean, I'm a wolf and half fairy, for god's sake. I'm past the point of being surprised by much in any of these worlds. This is Frayan, so maybe there aren't just fairies here. I look down at my shirt, which is now ripped in several places, and my jeans are just the same. I'm sure my hair is a right mess from the flight, and my stomach is still turning from it. I glance behind me, and the wings are gone, which is a slight relief.

"Who are you, and why did you just pick me up out of the forest like a toy?" I breathlessly demand, still not moving my eyes lower than the man's face because he is still very naked, and he doesn't seem to care one bit. "Though thank you. We did need a little help, it seems." He is a dragon who changes into a handsome man, who only smirks at me. This place has goddamn massive dragons. I think back to the fury on Lily's face when the dragon swooped down and stole me from right in front of her. Lily is going to search for me, and she is clearly mad from everything she said. But I also think back to my mother, who said she was a queen of one of the courts here in Frayan, and what Lily said confirmed that. I've just been thrown into a world full of dark secrets, with a crazy asshole at my side, a pixie that will no doubt abandon me the moment she can, and now there is a dragon.

"Jonas...long time no see," Josh states, offering Jonas a hand to shake, which he does. "Aren't you meant to be in Dragca, training to be a dragon guard?" So this man—no, dragon—is from that Dragca place Josh talked about.

"You know him?" I interject.

"Jonas is from Dragca, and a bit from Earth in a way. We needed his help back there, so I think we should say thank you and then get moving," Josh remarks, looking around at the purple land of trees we are in and the yellow grass that moves on its own under our feet. "Rick, Mich and Nath won't be far behind us. They will find a way in."

"I've already said thank you to the naked dragon," I say, shaking my head and getting frustrated as I don't want more people I care about coming to the land of crazy fairies. "I'm not going anywhere until someone explains how I had wings myself. Oh, and what Queen Winter did to get us stuck in Frayan, and how exactly we get back to Earth and to my sister."

"I don't have those answers. The royal seer of Dragca, who's one of my mums, said I needed to be here. Only, she gave me no other directions or what I am meant to do while I'm here. I have a house not far from here, and it is safe for now," Jonas replies to me, crossing those beefy arms over his naked chest. Dear god, does this guy spend all day working out?

"Does it have clothes for you to put on?" I sarcastically ask.

"Does me being naked bother you all that much?" he teases, and I glare at him, getting flustered because it damn well does bother me. Naked, very attractive guys would bother any girl.

"Keep your dragon dick to yourself, J, and lead the way to this house. Being out in the open isn't a great idea with that crazy queen looking for Adie," Josh growls, wrapping a possessive arm around my waist that I push off before stepping away.

"Don't go pretending you like me now, Josh," I remark, my hand automatically touching the bracelet that Nath gave me. I wish he was here because he would know what to do. So would Rick and Mich. Josh is the hot head of the pack and uses emotions to make decisions rather than logic.

"I'm not pretending anything. Did jumping through a magic portal to another world not prove anything to you about how I feel, Adie?" he asks, shaking his head at me like I'm the one in the wrong here, before walking to Jonas's side. Jonas smirks before running a hand through his icy white hair and turning around, leaving me a view of his perfect ass. Trapped in a random forest in Frayan with Josh and a naked dragon. This is definitely unexpected.

CHAPTER
THREE

"Come to me, wolf fate. I call you home. Come to me, child. I call you home..."

I nearly jump out of my skin when I hear the strange voice calling to me, the soft voice sounding like it is inches away from my ear. I stop, spinning around to look for the voice's owner, but we are alone, and there is nothing but the trees and leaves moving in the wind. There is no one here but me, Jonas, and Josh, who are silent as they walk through the forest that seems endless. Jonas swears he knows where he is going, and I don't have any reason to doubt him, consid-

22

ering he just saved Josh and me from that crazy woman. I look back to them just as the home Jonas must have been talking about comes into view. I breathe in the smells of the forest, trying to ignore how much my body itches to shift into my wolf so she can run around and enjoy this place.

My wolf might be relaxed, but I am certainly not. This is Frayan, the place I was born and the place I've been hidden from. If there was nothing to be scared of here, then why on Earth would my parents never tell me about it? Why would we have spent our entire lives on the run? I wish my mum and dad were here to tell me everything. The letter mum left me is useless now; it doesn't give me any answers that I seek. Then, there is the fact they weren't my biological parents in the first place, and my family comes from this place. I wonder if all the answers I want are here. But I can't risk staying here too long. That queen clearly wants me dead, and my sister is on Earth, and she needs me to bring her up.

"Home sweet home," Jonas almost sarcastically says as we get to a wooden lodge in the middle of the forest we have been walking through for a good hour. The dragon could have landed nearer, that's all I'm saying. Or not saying. I'm not stupid enough to try and fight a dragon. My wolf would be nothing more than a pretty snack, and I have no clue how to use my powers to defend myself. I'm exhausted from not only the walking, but everything that happened today. Somehow, I've lost my mother, developed new powers, been taken through a portal to another world, and now all this walking, all in one day. My eyes are barely staying open at this point.

I look up at the sky, where three moons have gradually appeared, each one the same size. They make the forest almost bright even now at night. I move my gaze back to Josh and Jonas, who thankfully found a blanket in the forest and wrapped it around his lower half. I've learnt Jonas is twenty-three, very energetic and a dragon guard in his final year of training from the world of Dragca. There is apparently a whole world full to the brim with dragons, and they have an academy for them to train. I would like to see it one day because it sounds pretty awesome—if I survive this place, that is.

As much as I'm scared and feeling lost…there is another part of me that is drawn to this place. The trees are so beautiful and calming to watch as they sway in the breeze, the soft wind blowing my hair around me. The place smells amazing, like a mix of a million flowers and pine trees. I just want to lie down and stare at this world and find out more about it. Everywhere is so bright, even though it is night and the sun has set. The millions of stars light up the sky, the light bouncing off the three moons I can see in a clearing of the trees. It's so very silent, which is strange for a forest. My wolf should be able to sense deer or rabbits nearby, or hear birds whistling, but there is nothing.

I was born here...I have a feeling we are in the Autumn court, but I might be wrong, and I don't want to think on that sad thought any longer. Thinking about the little I know of my past isn't going to help me find answers. My eyes drift over to Josh, and my thoughts drift to what he said about liking me. I can't stop thinking about it, but now really isn't the time to bring it up again.

"Jonas, do you know what court we are in?" I ask him as we climb up the few steps to the front door, which is next to a window with no curtains.

"It's the edge of the Autumn court, and over that way is the start of the Summer court," Jonas says, pointing to our right. "I travelled around a little since my mum never said which court I should be in to find you. Just that I had to find Josh and save the woman he is with. Real useful on this giant island."

"Why did you choose here then?" I ask him as he unlocks the door, and Josh is keeping an eye out around us. I doubt Lilyanne will find us here, but we can't be too careful.

"The Autumn court has the nicest people around, and it's not too overpopulated. The Summer court is dead; there is nothing and no one much living there since the sun doesn't apparently make it as hot as it used to. The Winter court is much the same, just pure ice, and people say it hasn't snowed for years. The land in those courts... it's like they are dead. The Spring court is packed with people, too many people for me to stay hidden. This court has some people, they just hide around in the tall trees and caves," Jonas explains, pushing the door open and holding it for me to go in first. "They even have villages hidden in the trees. The people say the queen knows of their existence, but she doesn't care much about them as long as they don't rebel against her."

"What happens when you go against her?" I ask as I step into the lounge, and they both follow me. Jonas locks the door and places the key on a ledge by the door and window.

"You end up dead, or she takes your power. She has crystals that can do that, and her home is covered in them. Only royals can stand against her, and she murdered them all years ago," he explains to me. "The people are too scared to stand against her, and I don't blame them."

"Not all of them are dead," I say on instinct, and I have no clue why I'm telling a virtual stranger who I am. I've got to keep silent and make sure I'm not found. Jonas looks at me wide-eyed, but I move to watch Josh as he lays Tay on a cushion on a wicker sofa in the room. He covers her with a blanket before pulling his jacket off and hanging it on the sofa. In this room are two wicker sofas with fur blankets hanging over them, a big fireplace and not much else. There are three other doors, and one of them is left open to the hallway at the back of the cabin. I rub my arms as I look around, and my gaze drifts back to Josh to find him watching me, his arms crossed and his eyes scrunched in a scowl.

"You've really got us in some trouble now, haven't you, Adie?" he mumbles almost softly, though there is an undertone that makes me shiver. The truth is, since I met his pack, I've caused nothing but a lot of trouble.

"My mother was Asteria and queen of the Autumn court," I tell them both, but it's more for Josh because he doesn't know anything, and he followed me here. Josh deserves the truth, and lies never get you anywhere. It's for myself, too. I need to say it out loud a few times so I can get used to the truth. It hurts that I only got to see my mother for a few moments, only to hold her as she died. Some might say it was a blessing that I got any moments with her at all. I just don't know how to take it as a blessing when it hurts so damn much to even think about it. I miss my sister. I miss Rick, Mich and Nath, which is madness because we have only been apart a few hours. I never knew how much I wanted a pack, a family, until now.

"Then you just became the most wanted person on Frayan," Jonas mutters and goes further into the room as I stare at Josh, wanting to know his thoughts. I never knew I cared so much about what Josh thinks...but I do. "Be right back," Jonas awkwardly states, looking between us before he disappears into one of the rooms. For a moment which seems to stretch forever, Josh just stares at me. I feel like my whole body burns to see him move closer to me, to simply have him close enough to know he isn't going to run away. I want

Josh, which is a new thought to me. When he moves, a nervous breath escapes my lips, and I don't dare move under the pressure of his gaze. Josh stops right in front of me, looking furious, I think, and something else at the same time, which I can't read.

"I can't use my demon powers here. I can't protect you like you need me to. It should have been any of the others to come with you, just not me," Josh quietly says, not sounding like Josh at all. I didn't expect him to say that, and for a second, I'm lost for words.

"I want you here," I say, my voice full of unspoken emotion I can't explain, but it feels like it clogs my throat up anyway. Josh lifts his hand, drifting it down my cheek until he cups my face. His warm hand pressed against my skin settles my emotions in some ways and stirs them in others that I never expected. When Nath and Rick kissed me, I felt like this. Like I never wanted the contact to stop.

"I will protect you. I don't know why, but I've always wanted to protect you, Adie. Always," he tells me, staring deeply into my eyes. My hands shake as I place them on his shirt, spreading my fingers out across his chest. I feel his heart beating

29

so fast under my palm as I stare right into his dark eyes. They may be so dark, but in the darkness is soft little dots of blue. I find myself wanting to stare into his eyes for hours, counting the blue dots, committing them to memory so I never forget.

"Always?" I ask, tilting my head to the side a little bit as I take in his words. "Always is a long time, Josh. Especially for someone you don't like."

"I'm good at pretending I don't like you, when the truth is—"

"Hey, so my mum—" Jonas comes into the room at the worst possible moment. I practically jump away from Josh on instinct, and Jonas only smirks as he comes up to us, carrying two plastic bags under his arms. This time he has clothes on and a big white handled sword on his hip in a holder. "As I was saying, my mum knows the future, and she packed you these bags."

"Thank you, Jonas. I owe you a lot, mate," Josh says as he takes his bag, and I also take mine.

"Yes, thank you," I tell him, knowing we would be in a different situation altogether if Jonas wasn't here.

"Don't thank me yet. Mum said I have to keep you alive, and that isn't over yet. I'm taking the first guard, and we should swap halfway through the night, Josh," Jonas suggests, placing his hand on his sword.

"Good idea," Josh is quick to agree. I'm pretty sure it's the fact I'm a girl that they have forgotten my existence in the guard duty plans.

"I can do a shift; I have my wolf senses. I would smell and hear someone a mile or so off," I remind them, needing to tell them and actually help. I'm no princess in a castle that can't protect herself. My wolf is strong, and I trust her completely to save us both.

"Not a good idea. We should keep you hidden, and you must wear a cloak with your hood up while we are out," Jonas suggests. "Hair colour seems to be important around here, and I've never seen anyone with as bright red hair as you have. Everyone has streaks of colour, depending on which court they were born in. They never have a full head of vibrant colour hair."

"Why didn't Lilyanne have bright hair then?" Josh asks.

"She isn't like the royals, that's what everyone says. I don't know much else," Jonas replies. "But even if we hide Adelaide's hair, she should stay hidden."

"Why?" I ask.

"Someone might recognise you. I'm sure Lilyanne has spies everywhere," Josh interrupts to say, and I guess he has a point. I'm going to find a way to help somehow though, because sitting in here all day doing nothing isn't happening. I can't hide in a cabin with Josh and Jonas for the rest of my life.

"You owe me a drink, by the way," Jonas says, laughing as he pats Josh's shoulder, and Josh grins at him before Jonas heads out of the room, locking the door behind him.

"Go and rest, Adie. Tomorrow will no doubt be tiring," Josh suggests, and I nod, once again lost for words. I feel Josh's eyes on me as I head to the corridor until he can't see me. I open a door, finding a small bedroom with a single bed that doesn't look slept on, so I doubt this is Jonas's room. I close the door, and without even getting changed, I lie on the bed. I'm so tired my eyes close almost instantly, and the next minute, I'm fast asleep.

CHAPTER
FOUR
ADELAIDE

Light flickers into my eyes, disappearing into the darkness every so often before coming back. It's soothing for a while, lulling me back into a deep sleep where wolves run after me, and I laugh because I want them to chase me. They are my pack after all. They would never hurt me. Owls fly above us in the trees, and children's laughter tickles my ears in my wolf form. Everything is so perfect, so peaceful and happy that I'm happy to ignore the world for a few more moments of these dreams. After more light flickers across my eyes, each time a little longer, I'm forced to pull my tired eyes open. I roll onto my side, looking at the grey curtains blowing in the wind.

Every so often, it blows far enough out to let some light in before collapsing back to the window. For a tiny second, it just feels perfectly relaxing, until my wolf reminds me that I'm not on Earth anymore. This is Frayan, though she seems to like it here. I'm itching to shift, but I'm well aware that shifting anytime soon isn't the best option I have or what I need to be worrying about. I stretch out as I stand up, knowing I must have slept the entire night, and I didn't wake up even once.

"Come to me, wolf fate, before it is too late. Come to me...come to me..."

I JUMP out of my skin, a low growl leaving my lips as I spin around, looking for the voice I heard. It's a woman, I think, and her voice is oddly soothing if not a little familiar. This is the second time I've heard it now, and the first, I chalked off as nothing, but this is getting to be too much to pretend didn't happen. The voice said the exact same thing both times, and what the heck is a wolf fate? I'm not sure where it wants me to go anyway.

I shake my head when I realise that I'm not going to find answers searching this empty room; clearly no one is here. There isn't anyone in the house that I can sense, though Josh is just outside. Who knows what kind of magic Frayan has; maybe the very island is whispering to me? Or maybe I am actually losing what is left of my rational thinking. *Come on, Adelaide, islands don't talk.*

I pick up the plastic bag off the floor and see a towel with a note on it that says the shower is across the hallway. After making my bed, I leave the bag on it and take the towel with me across the hallway. I open the other door, where there is a stone shower unlike anything I've seen before, but the toilet looks the same as they do on Earth, if not a slightly older model. *Small bonus, I see.* I use the toilet after locking the door, and then I take my clothes off. I pause in utter shock as I get a look at myself in the mirror. My stomach, hips and ribs are covered in tattoos of green vines with red and blue roses snaking around me. They wrap around my stomach and back and all the way up to my ribs where they stop. I remember my body burning when I came through the portal, and this must have been the reason. I lift my hair, seeing two vines on the sides of my neck, and they meet at the back of my neck before going down my back. As I stare at the markings, they almost seem to move on their own.

I drop my hair and cover my face with my hands, taking a deep breath before dropping them. This is what I was always meant to look like. The blue wings I have, which I assume only come out when I use my powers, are meant to be mine. The red and blue must be part of who I am too, though I don't fully understand it all. The red I assume is from my mother, the queen of the Autumn court. I don't know much about my father other than the mumbles Asteria said before she died. My mum's letter didn't make much sense other than saying he was an alpha or something. It would explain where my wolf comes from if he was a wolf shifter. Asteria talked about him being powerful, but she never mentioned him being the king of the Autumn court. Can you have both king and queen of a court? Or is it just one ruler? I stop re-running a million questions in my head, knowing it isn't getting me anywhere, just as someone knocks the door a few times. I wrap the towel around me before pulling the door open a little bit, seeing Josh on the other side.

"Are you okay?" he asks, his eyes widening ever so slightly as he runs them up my legs, past my towel until he meets my eyes and remembers to carry on talking. It's rather sweet, even if everything about Josh makes me nervous. Something has changed about him. He doesn't seem so angry and lost here, and I want to know why. "The shower is weird to use, so I thought you might need some help."

"Yes, I actually don't have a clue how to turn it on," I say, pulling the door further open and shutting it behind him as he comes in. He goes to the shower, and I watch as he waves a hand over a crystal on the wall. Purple water falls out of the holes in the top of the stone, crashing on the stone floor. Even the water smells nice in this place.

"Jonas explained to me how crystals seem to be a massive part of the Frayan way of life. We use crystals for a lot back on Earth, but not to this extent. We more use them for protection wards. The crystals have actually changed the colour of the water, the trees and even grass. I don't know why, but it somehow makes this place seem like pure magic. That's saying a lot considering I was brought up in a castle full of magical beings," Josh explains to me. I gently place my hand on his shoulder, and he turns to me.

"Thank you. Not just for the help with the shower, but for being here. For helping me when I was lost in the power I created. I couldn't let go, I didn't want to, and you helped me. I will always owe you a debt for that and for coming here with me," I softly tell him, knowing I've wanted to thank him since the moment I woke up here.

"When I first got my demon powers, I thought I was invincible. My adoptive mum, Winter, tried to warn me that I had to learn to control the power before it controlled me. I never understood what she meant, so I didn't listen to her. I didn't listen to anyone," he humourlessly laughs, and I feel like he isn't even aware I'm here as he tells me this story. "I turned seventeen, and I was bored out of my mind. The castle is always so busy and full, but when you are an outsider like me, it can feel like the emptiest place in the world. Winter warned me not to tap into my demon powers, and I had enough of listening to her, though a part of me loved her like a mother and knew she was only protecting me. Her mates grew angry with my attitude, as did Nath, Rick and Mich who told me I needed to calm down. I thought I knew best, and I didn't. I went to a party alone, and I was kissing a human girl not long after being there. I didn't even know her name at the time, but I lost control of my powers. I literally took her soul, destroying her and killing her in the process."

"It was an accident," I say, hearing the pain and grief in his tone. I want to hug him, tell him that he was a kid and that his demon powers had been supressed for so long that they just exploded out. I can see Rick, Nath and Mich don't blame him. They love him and know it was an accident.

"And since then, I've been nothing but angry, out of control and a monster. The half of me that is literally from hell is impossible to control. Winter has a quarter demon blood, and she thought I was the same as her. That I would be able to control it as she does. I couldn't, not without feeling like the other half, my angel soul, was dying. That is until I came here," he tells me, his voice cracked and broken. The falling shower water, the sound of it hitting the stone as the room slowly becomes steamy, does nothing to hide the way he is feeling.

"Why are you telling me this?" I ask him, because I don't understand. He has never opened up to me, and I have the feeling he doesn't just tell anyone his past. Josh is a private person, a closed book with a nasty bite at times. Despite that, I want to be near him all the time. Maybe I'm just a sucker for punishment.

"My demon side feels gone here, and for once, I feel free," he gently tells me, his dark eyes watching me closely. "I don't have to force myself to keep everyone at a distance here." I try to pretend he doesn't mean me, that I'm reading his emotions and the way he is looking at me wrong. Because if I let myself think he is really looking at me that way and thinking of me like that, it's a dangerous slope into falling for him. Josh would be easy to fall in love with, but it would be like jumping headfirst into a deep lake, unaware of the large rocks that could kill you beneath the icy, beautiful water.

"You have been nicer since we got here," I remark, trying to add humour to the tense and confusing situation.

"Was I that much of an asshole before?" he asks with a smirk on his lips. I grin at him as I nod, and he turns to fully face me. Slowly, he places both his hands on my cheeks and, before saying a word, he leans down and kisses me. The kiss is slow at the start, both of us exploring each other before he deepens the kiss. If I'm going to jump into the lake, I might as well do it quickly and pretend it isn't going to hurt. I slide my hands through his silky hair as his arms wrap around me, pressing my body against his. One thing for sure, Josh knows how to kiss. I'm almost sad when he pulls back, staring down at me with clear longing to do more than just kiss. "I never wanted to get close to you before...because of what happened in my past. That side of me, I never wanted, and now it feels like I can go after what I want."

"Which is?" I ask, and he ever so softly kisses me for an answer before letting me go. "You know the answer, Adie." I watch him with a big smile on my lips as he goes to the door. "One more thing, did you always have those tattoos? They are stunning."

"Not until I came here, but maybe I was always meant to have them," I tell him, placing my hand into the purple water to feel how warm it is.

"They suit you," Josh says with a wink before opening the door and leaving the room. I lock the door before leaving my towel on the side and getting into the shower, letting the warm water try to cool me down. Even though we are lost in Frayan, I feel like I found a piece of my soul with Josh. And I never would have found it if we hadn't been forced to come here.

To come home.

CHAPTER
FIVE
ADELAIDE

After a quick shower, I towel dry my hair and sit down on my bed, pulling the bag towards me. I open it and find a note right on top of the pile of clothes. I open the note up, which is written on silver paper with a dragon symbol at the bottom.

To Adelaide Autumn, heir to the Autumn court of Frayan,

I have foreseen your arrival in Frayan for many years, and I do hope my son has helped you escape a daunting fate so that you may have a chance of seeing this.

43

When the time comes, send my son home, and we will return with the Dragca army. My queen, Isola Pendragon, and her four kings will aid you in your war in exchange for a promise of peace between our realms.
A Fray promise is unbreakable.
For peace is all we strive towards, and I believe you will want the same outcome.

Be safe, Adelaide.
I am looking forward to meeting you in the future.
Do not let the prophecy destroy you both, for it would be a sorrowful ending to such a wretched war.

Forever watching,
The royal seer of Dragca,
Melody Pendragon.

I PUT THE NOTE DOWN, feeling strange that seers exist in some dragon world, and she is watching me, knowing my actions before I've even made them. What did she mean about not letting the prophecy destroy us both? Me and Josh? I really need to find out what the hell this prophecy says that I've heard whispered about more than once now. The book mum left me spoke about it as well, and this note just means it's important. Why else would this Melody mention it and send her son to help me.

I know sitting here in a towel isn't going to get me any of the answers I want, only getting up and moving is going to do that. I'm in Frayan, where all of this started and where I was born. All of the truth—be it good or bad—is here. I open the bag, finding three outfits and a long thick red cloak. All the clothes are black leather, and there is a cool leather jacket at the bottom of the bag. I don't know if it's creepy or cool that she got everything the right size.

I pull on the clothes, doing up the belt at the top of the leather leggings. I look between the leather jacket and the cloak, wondering why she gave me a choice of two coats. I'm thinking a cloak will fit in more with the people here. I pick it up, sliding my arms through the gaps and clipping up the few buttons at the top. They are silver clips with leaves engraved into them.

I pull my hair out, which is still a little damp, and use the hairbrush out of the bag to brush out the knots until it falls straight down my back. I put everything back into the bag before pulling on my socks and boots and leaving my room. I find Jonas and Josh in the living room, and they both look my way as I come in.

They have similar clothes on today, black leather trousers and tops, with black cloaks wrapped around their thick shoulders, though it looks out of place on Jonas with his contrasting white hair and pale complexion. Josh, with his wavy black hair and tanned skin, seems to be really well-suited in the all black look. Though they somewhat remind me of Harry Potter and Draco Malfoy dressed like this, and the thought brings a smile to my lips.

"Here, I made breakfast for you," Jonas says, pointing at a plate of fruit and cooked meat with some cheese. I doubt Draco Malfoy would be making me breakfast, so maybe he isn't the mean one of the two. *Yeah, that's definitely Josh.* I sit down on the empty seat in the room, picking up the plate and smiling at Jonas in appreciation. I could see us being friends in the future, he has that like-able quality about him. Though he is a little flirty, I can sense he more admires the idea of me than the actual me.

"Thanks," I say, looking at the strange fruit I don't recognise at all. It's pink for one, and it looks a little like a mix between an apple and an orange, yet there are pink spikes on the skin. I suppose I shouldn't expect the food would be the same here, but for some reason, I expected to see a full English breakfast on the table, and I haven't a clue why.

"Where is Tay?" I ask because Josh is sitting on the sofa she was on last night.

"Still sleeping. I thought she might have woken up by now," Josh replies. "I thought she would be more comfortable in a bed than out here."

"She is from Frayan, so perhaps it's a magic thing," I explain to Josh, who nods but looks annoyed that he didn't know that already as he narrows his eyes. I pick on the cheese and meat, which is really nice, as Josh turns to Jonas.

"So how did you get here?" he asks, clearly not wanting to ask me more about the secrets I've been keeping.

"King Atticus of Earth and King Dagan of Dragca have been doing tests on crystals to open portals. It's been years, but they finally figured out a way to make a small, temporary portal. The only issue they found is that it takes two years, possibly longer, to charge a stone for one trip here. I just about made it through the portal before it shut behind me," Jonas explains to us. God, there are a lot of kings to keep up with. I'm going to need a history lesson on all these people when we have some spare time. I wish there was a book on Earth and Dragca's shared history, especially the times of the war.

"There is a chance Winter has some of these stones then. Rick, Nath and Mich could get here to help us—" Josh remarks, and my heart beats all the louder for hearing there is a chance I could see my pack again.

"There isn't a way back though, and I don't know if they made more stones. All the old Fray portals are gone," Jonas explains. "There used to be many according to my history teacher at Dragca Academy."

"The portals opened in the war, for only a little bit, but still..." Josh counters.

"I've heard that was because it was a special day. I can't remember why, but it only happens once every two thousand years. That's why they wanted to make portals, and they did so much research," Jonas replies.

"We should ask around; the people might know something we don't. I don't want Rick, Nath and Mich coming here and getting stuck because of a one-way stone ticket. If we can figure out a way back, it solves all the problems. Lilyanne can have this world, and she won't have to kill me," I say, and they both look at me like I've lost the plot.

"It's where you were born, Adelaide. You are an heir, a royal Fray. A protector of the people—"

"People I don't know and have never known. My sister, though not by blood, is back on Earth, and she needs me. I can't fix all of Frayan, and all this place has given me is misery. My biological parents are dead because of this world, and my parents who brought me up spent their lives running from this place. Why would I want to save somewhere I don't know? People who didn't help when my parents were killed? Frayan lost me everything when I was just a baby, and now I'm meant to what? Fight for a world that doesn't want or know me?" I rant, knowing my emotions have somewhat gotten the better of me.

"You need to at least see what you're walking away from, Adie," Josh gently suggests. "Once Fray go back to Earth, they lose their powers for some reason. You need to see the world you are going to run from before you leave. Frayan didn't cause you misery, Lilyanne did. This world cannot be held to blame for the actions of one."

"I'm not their saviour," I warn him, shaking my head. "For heaven's sake, I can't even lift a sword, let alone fight to win a throne. It's not who I am."

"How do you know that?" Josh replies, and he has me there. I don't know. "How do you know who you are? As far as I know, all the truths of your life have been thrown at you so rapidly, in such a short time, that no one could blame you for freaking out. All I'm saying is don't give up on a world you don't know. This is your home, your fate."

"Everything happens for a reason, be it good or bad," Jonas says, the statement seeming to fix itself into my head. "My mum always said that to me. And she would know; she sees the future."

"We aren't going to get answers sitting here," I say, standing up and needing the pressure and attention to be off me.

"The village isn't far. Let's go," Jonas says, standing up, and Josh offers me a hand.

"Whether or not you're their saviour, you'll always have me by your side. You aren't alone," Josh tells me. "You have a pack, remember?"

"Pack is family," I whisper, sliding my hand into his. It doesn't change anything. I can't be what the people need. I'd only disappoint them.

"And family always have your back," Josh replies. I just wish I could believe him. Right now, it feels like I'm leading my pack into the most dangerous situation of their lives.

And I want them here. *What does that say about me?*

CHAPTER
SIX

RICK

Every time the clock moves, it just seems to remind me that I am powerless to do anything but wait, listening to the council try to figure out a plan. Listen to Winter, my dad, my uncle and everyone in my family fret over the right thing to do. Atti went to Dragca with Winter to get something, but no one is making any sense about what it is. Uncle J suggested we go and train to take our minds off Adelaide, but with the mood I'm in...I'd end up losing my temper. Dad thinks giving me his Oreos, despite how much he doesn't want to share them, will make me happy. I guess he got his answer when I threw them across the room. Mich and Nath are as silent as I am. Our pack is split up, and there is nothing we can do about it.

I cross my arms and walk to the window of the room, looking down at the courtyard below. There is a class out there of wolves running in perfect circles to my aunt's instruction. I recognise one little brown wolf at the back who, even though she is smaller than the others, is keeping up with them. Adelaide would be proud of her sister. I've been too much of a coward to go and tell Sophie that her sister is in trouble, because I know she will ask what I'm going to do to save her. Right now? I don't have an answer for that. Every second Adelaide and Josh could be in more trouble, and I'm stuck here on Earth. Even Tay is with them, and who knows what travelling through a portal could have done to her? I know it was not Winter's fault this all happened, but I still struggle to talk to her since we got back to the castle. I see Winter, and I can only envision the moment she shook hands with Adelaide, and I lost her. I lost the woman I'm falling in love with.

Mich and Nath are just as stressed as I am as we wait outside the council room, an hour after hearing Winter and Atti were back from Dragca. Winter swears that she has found something,

something that will help us, but that's all we know. The council have been told of all major developments, including us possibly going to Frayan to save Adelaide. For all we know, we could be starting a war with Frayan. A war Winter and everyone here would have to fight to save me, their heir and prince. At least that is my title until the baby Winter is carrying is born. In some ways, I will be happy to not have that title hanging over me. I've been the prince since the war, stuck in meeting after meeting until I resigned my place at the council table to go with my pack on our mission with the hunters. That is the only good thing that has come out of my life so far: The Hunter's Organisation was destroyed.

Everyone is free, and the human news is blown up with horror stories we recorded and made sure were posted everywhere on the internet. We hope the humans will come to the conclusion working with the supernaturals is a better option than hunting and hurting them. The ball is in their court now.

The door to the waiting room is pulled open as Uncle J steps out, nodding his head at Nath and Mich who bow their heads in respect for their king, though Uncle J hates when people do that, especially people close to the family. I don't do it mainly because Uncle J hits me around the head when I do, telling me family don't bow.

"She didn't mean it, you know. Winter loves you like her own child and would never hurt you or your mate," Uncle J tells me as he comes and stops right in front of me, his arms crossed against his checked shirt. He always hated when Winter was in any kind of trouble. He always hated when I was too. "Winter hasn't stopped crying since this all happened. Her hormones are making this a million times worse. If you love her, please tell the lass you don't hate her."

"I don't hate her for it. I just need to get into Frayan and to Adelaide," I mutter, rubbing my face with my palms. "If anything happens to Adelaide, I don't know how I would survive it."

"You love the lass, don't you?" Uncle J asks, and I catch how Mich and Nath are quick to listen in.

"Seeing as I haven't had a chance to tell her that yet, I'm not telling you."

"That's a yes," Uncle J laughs, patting my shoulder hard enough he nearly knocks me over. Damn alpha uncles. "Love is tricky but rewarding in ways you won't ever understand until you understand."

"That doesn't make sense," I tell him.

"It will, lad," Uncle J states, grinning at me.

"I'm worried about what being in Frayan will do to Josh. Any change makes his powers react badly," I say.

"I never liked the lad; I'm not going to lie. That is until I saw him save his pack by walking through lightning to get their girl. I admire that strength and the bravery it took. Seems Adelaide has made him more of a man than we ever could do. Whatever Frayan does to Josh's powers, he is Adelaide's to control now," Uncle J says, shaking his head.

"She pushes and pushes him sometimes. I think he likes it though," I confide.

"Winter used to do the same to me. There was a time I hated how much I loved Winter, and I tried to walk away. I didn't get very far." Uncle J laughs as I chuckle. I can't imagine he did. The door to the council room opens as Uncle J lowers his hand from my shoulder. Winter and Atti walk out together, looking nervous as they meet my eyes.

"This is how you are going to get to Adelaide," Winter says as she comes right up to us. My pack quickly come over, watching her with me as she opens a tiny box in her hands. Inside, there are five stones resting on white fabric. Each one of them is a purple colour, and they glow slightly.

"We have been trying to figure out a way to get to Frayan for many years. I never wanted to send Adelaide to her, because I know that she is evil and that I'd be sentencing an innocent to death. Adelaide is in grave danger, and part of me does not want to send you to Frayan because that danger will become your own. I know I can also not hold you back, so these are yours. I will keep two of them for when you need us to follow you," Winter says, a sob catching in her throat. I step forward, wrapping my arms around Winter as she softly cries on my shoulder for a little while.

"I don't blame you, Winter. You are my mum in every sense, and you are the kindest, most pure-hearted person I know. I will save Adelaide; it is my fate, and then I will bring her to you somehow. I want my mum to properly meet the woman I know is my mate. Please don't feel guilty, this is not your fault," I whisper to her, well aware everyone in the room can hear me.

"I love you. I can't lose both my sons in Frayan, so you have to come back, or I'm coming to you,"

Winter states, pulling back and wiping her eyes as Atti wraps an arm around her shoulder.

"Good job. She might actually sleep now. You're a good son," Atti whispers into my mind and grins at me.

"You can't follow them. The castle, the people and everybody here needs their queen. You're pregnant, and your child will need you," Uncle J tells her. "I want to protect my nephew too, but sometimes we have to let him go and be the man we have brought him up to be."

"I have no doubt our son and his pack will save this woman and come back to us," dad says as he comes into the room with Dabriel following and walks over to me. He pulls me into a tight hug, holding me closely before letting me go so that Winter and Uncle J can hug me too. I fist bump Atti's waiting fist and nod once to Dabriel with a smile. Nath and Mich say their goodbyes as well, though I know Nath has already spoken to his mother and said a teary goodbye.

"Winter, Uncle J and in fact all of you, you brought me up to be strong, to be loyal and to always put family first. They are my pack, and I have to go save them. I know we will see each other again; I'm not worried about that," I say, knowing I will find a way to bring Adelaide back. Somehow.

"We will always find a way. If you need help, if you need anything, find a way to tell me," Winter firmly says, hugging me one more time before letting me go.

"I'm working on a way to send brief witch touched letters through a tiny portal. I expect we will be able to contact you soon," Atti says, and it gives me hope we won't be on our own in this world we have never been to.

"Are you ready?" I ask Mich and Nath. I've never been the alpha that leads, not until this point. I've always let my pack be equal to me in everything, and never asserting my dominance. Not until I had something worth fighting for, that is. I will leave my family to save my pack, the people that rely on me. It is what an alpha does. Mich and Nath stand tall, and I know that they will fight till the end for our pack. We have to do this, and we have to win. Adie and Josh are waiting for us.

"Take it," Dad says, pulling out a long red sword from his holder before offering it to me. "You are my heir, and you are going to war. This will help."

"Thank you," I tell him, accepting the sword I know he loves a lot. I take out my current sword from the holder and slide this one into it instead. Dad takes my old sword off me before stepping back to Winter's side. Nath and Mich have daggers and have packed enough things to keep us alive for a while, no matter what we face in there. The only issue is Mich won't be able to use his witch magic to move us around, not unless he has seen the place before. It's one of the limits of his power.

"Are you sure there is nothing else we can do?" Winter asks as I pick up one of the stones, and Nath does the same, followed by Mich.

"We have everything we could need," I say, because Winter packed us a bag full of weapons, blood, medical supplies and food enough to feed an army. We will be able to survive there for quite a while. I am hoping we can find Adie and Josh without much trouble. Then we can figure out the rest to do.

"You have to break the crystals. I would suggest throwing them on the ground," Atti explains. "They take two years to make, and we won't have new ones ready for another year." Winter starts crying when she hears this, and

Uncle J sweeps her up into his arms as she watches me.

"I will tell the baby all about his brothers. Or her brothers," Winter says to me.

"Take lots of photos for me, mum," I reply to her, and she nods, smiling as she rests a hand on her bump.

"It's a promise," she whispers with a big smile. "I love you, and good luck," Winter says as she wipes away tears. I look once more at my pregnant stepmum, wishing I could be here for just a moment to meet my new brother or sister. I know that they will be well looked after by my dad, uncle and Winter's other mates. We will find a way back; I have to tell myself that to leave. I just have to save Adelaide and Josh first. I don't say anything else as I turn around, knowing we just need to leave as soon as we can. I stand in a line with Nath and Mich.

"Ready?" Nath asks, and I know he is still feeling guilty that Adelaide was in the hunter base in the first place. Their date didn't go to plan, and there is nothing I can say to make him feel better. I can't read Mich, though I've never been able to. He is a brother to me in every sense, but a closed book all the same.

"I am," Mich states, holding his head high, and I nod with a smile. With my pack, we can do anything.

"Good luck!" Atti shouts at us as, in unison, we throw the crystals onto the ground. They smash into dozens of little pieces which do nothing for a moment as I frown at them. Suddenly all the little pieces pull together, slamming into each other and making bright light which expands into a portal. The portal stretches, in a matter of moments, into a portal big enough for a human to go through. I don't wait or look back as we run into the portal, one by one, falling out into the field on the other side. Nath and Mich fall out next to me, rolling away a little, and I frown when I see Nath roll into the legs of someone.

I jump up quickly, spinning round to see that we are surrounded by guards that don't look friendly with their swords near my neck. They wear black metal uniforms, with black crystals pressed into their armour, their helmets covering their faces. The crystals almost seem to glow as they point their swords at us, and I scent they are Fray, though each one of them scents a little differ-ent, and none like Adelaide or Nath. Nath stands up, rubbing his head and pushing his hair out of the way. The blond now has blue in it, just like he had as a child until he dyed it to hide from the hunters.

"Welcome to Frayan. I have been expecting you," a sweet-sounding woman says as Mich and Nath come close to my side, a warning growl coming from them both that my wolf wants to join. I turn around to see the woman that spoke, who has a long black gown on, her strawberry blonde hair pulled up into a tight bun, and her features are somewhat cold and cruel. She wears a crown made of black stones much like the stones the guards have on their amour. I'm taking a wild guess this is the queen that Winter warned us about. She is the one that Adie was sent to.

"Who are you?" Nath asks before I can say anything. We are in big trouble now.

"Right now? I'm the person you need to beg to keep you alive," the woman says. She clicks her fingers, and the guards all rush towards us. "Adelaide doesn't need three lovers; one wouldn't be missed, would it?" she laughs as I growl.

Don't fight them. She must have Adie and Josh. We need her to take us to them, I tell my pack through our bond. The guards are quick to hand cuff us and hold us by our arms in front of the queen. She walks over to me, grabbing my chin with her hand, digging her nails into my cheek. "My name is Queen Lilyanne, and I do look forward to seeing Adelaide die to try and save you."

"You underestimate her—and us," I warn her.

"We will see," she replies with a laugh before walking away, and we are dragged with her.

My feet crunch against the autumn leaves that sprinted across the ground. Here they do not look like those from home; they look like leaves that have been painted purple by children. Everything about this place feels like I've dropped into a fairy tale. The yellow grass is so odd to me, but there's something so soothing about the way all the colours seem to mix together. It's almost like this is a natural way to be. I look up into the sky and grab my hood to make sure it doesn't fall down. The sun is more of an orange colour here, and the blue sky almost looks purple. It's not as cloudy today, but it feels a bit colder than it did yesterday.

I glance to my right where Josh is holding my

hand, walking next to my side. He now has a black cloak on, the hood pulled up to hide his face. He seems so easy in this place, like he was meant to come here. I know I was born here, but I still feel odd. I feel like an outsider in a place that I'm guessing is meant to be my home.

"Are you okay?" Josh asks me, like he can sense I am watching him. I take a deep breath and turn away, looking towards the village that is coming into view. It almost spills out of a cave, the many stalls and people just appearing out of nowhere. The trees do well to hide the village, and the large hill above the cave must hide it from view. Everyone seems to wear a mixture of different coloured cloaks, making everything seem so much brighter inside the cave, the lights reflecting off all the colours. The many stalls seem to be selling a wide variety of fruits and vegetables and many other things I don't recognise. The people don't look our way though as we walk towards them.

"I am okay. This is just a different world to get used to," I finally answer him back. Jonas looks back at us from where he is walking far ahead. He pauses to wait for us near the entrance of the cave, which smells like a mixture of people that I'm not used to scenting. I guess this is what Frayan people smell like.

"Maybe we can find some books on Frayan history. There might be something about your parents, but for now, we should focus on portals," Josh suggests, looking at the stores as we pass them, following Jonas, who clearly knows where he is going. He even waves at a few people as we pass them, and I try not to stare at how strange the people are here. For one, they have bright colours in their hair, many orange and blue streaked through brown and blonde. Children run by us, my cloak swinging into the air as they go past, their laughter filling my ears. There are a few stalls that are selling books and scrolls as we go past, and I keep a note of them to go back later.

"Good idea," is all I manage to say to Josh as I'm taking in everything around us, and he seems lost in this too. It's like we have gone back a few hundred years on Earth, to a time when people wore long dresses and cloaks. Where little villages like this were normal and not so strange. I do spot some human things for sale, an old radio and a globe that has seen better days, on one table.

"The worlds are all connected; sometimes things pass through. I was told that, many years ago, people would come and go from the worlds like it was nothing more than travelling," Jonas explains to us as we stop to let some people pass.

The cave opens up the more we travel into it, revealing all the crystal formations on the walls and surrounding the little houses above the market. There are so many different colours here, making the simple cave just feel so alive. I don't know the name of the crystals, but they don't look like anything I've ever seen before. There are lights high in the sky that reflect off the crystals so they make the cave brighter. Whatever I think of Frayan, I will always believe it to be extremely beautiful. I wonder if my parents ever stood where I am right now, if they looked over this village and saw it to be as beautiful as I do.

"This way," Jonas says, nodding his head towards some steps leading up to the houses by the looks of it. I move to walk in front of Josh as the pathway is narrow, and he lets my hand go so we can climb up the steps. We come up to a row of cave houses with yellow wooden doors, and the doors have different symbols etched onto the front of them. We pass two with snowflakes on the door, and then Jonas stops outside a door with a leaf symbol on it. He knocks a few times, and we wait in silence until the door is pulled open by a little girl. Jonas immediately kneels down to her level, and whatever look he has on his face makes her grin widely. Her wild brown hair has streaks of red littered through it, the brown matching her bright eyes. She has a strange orange dress on, which I would call a tunic with a fabric belt holding it together in the middle. From the looks of her dirty bare feet, I'd say she doesn't often wear shoes.

"The dragon is back, mama!" the little girl shouts into the house, only looking back for a second before fixing her eyes on Jonas. "Will you make it snow again? Or make me some of those ice cups to play with? Please! Please!"

"Of course, little Winnie. I am a servant to your demands," Jonas says and makes her laugh just as a woman comes to stand behind her. She has light brown hair, but the ends are a fiery red colour, and her brown eyes watch all of us with caution before going back to Jonas. She also has a tunic on, though hers is brown in colour, and it wraps around her tightly at the top, flowing out into a dress which just touches the ground, hiding her shoes.

"Jonas, you never said you had friends before,"

she says, her accent unfamiliar and strange to me, but I focus on how she doesn't sound like she trusts us one bit. I'm not sure this woman is going to be much help.

"I'm sorry to intrude, especially after how much you have helped me settle into Frayan in the first place. But my friends need to ask you some questions about Frayan that I don't have the answers to. They know little to nothing about this world," Jonas explains. "Adie, Josh, this is Darla. Darla, my friends mean you no harm, they are just new." Darla watches us closely, and I itch to lower my hood, to reveal more of myself to her so she will see I'm no harm. I still remember that Queen Lily is out there looking for me, and I have to be careful now. A gush of wind blows my hood back a little, a few strands of my hair falling out, and her eyes widen as she stares at me, looking like she has seen a ghost as I hide myself again.

"If you go with Winnie and take her to the market to get some new herbs, I don't see why I cannot try to answer some of your friends' questions," Darla finally says, coming to the conclusion that she trusts Jonas enough to talk to us. I'm interested to know why she looked at me that way.

"Perfect deal," Jonas says, winking at her, and

she blushes. Despite the fact Jonas is young enough to be her son, he is clearly a charmer. Winnie grabs Jonas's hand, dragging him off down the steps behind us, and Darla nods her head to the inside of her house as she keeps the door open for us. I walk past her, straight into the little home they have. There isn't much, just a few benches with fur hanging over them, facing a fireplace. The fireplace is lit, with a kettle on a rack above it. There are cups on top of the fire place, along with a selection of different bottles.

"Please sit. Would you both like a warm drink?" Darla asks, shutting the door. I lower my hood, looking back to her as her eyes widen once again, only this time she doesn't hide her shock as she goes a little pale. She slowly walks over to me, but Josh steps in front of me, lowering his own hood as he does.

"If you harm her or tell anyone we were here, you will live to regret it. Understood?" Josh threatens, and I step to his side, grabbing his arm.

"I would never harm her or tell a soul of her existence if she is who I believe she is," Darla is quick to reply, looking very scared of Josh. Though Josh scares everyone, so I'm not that shocked.

"Who do you think I am?" I ask as she turns to

look at me. She comes closer, picking up some of my bright red hair and stepping back before bowing her head.

"I met your mother only once, but you are the image of her. You are a royal, and you are *not* safe here," she tells me. I know I'm not, but I wonder if she thinks the same thing as I do. I also know I look like my mother, Asteria. It hurts to even think back to her and how she died in my arms yesterday. I was powerless to save her, and avenging her by killing Mr. Graves didn't make me feel better. He should have died slower, not burning into dust like he did. At least he screamed...and I'm somewhat happy to know he died in pain.

"Why aren't I safe?" I ask her, and Josh chooses to step back a little. Still close enough to protect me if I need it.

"Queen Lilyanne killed all the royals, and she will not stop," Darla says in a hushed whisper, like she is too scared to even say it out loud. If everyone is too scared of Lily, then how am I meant to get them to side with me to fight her? I can't fight her on my own.

"I know she is looking for me. I need answers; please, will you help me?" I ask. I want the truth, the reality of everything I don't understand.

"Yes, you are the heir to my court. The Autumn court and all its subjects are yours," she says, bowing her head once more. I step closer despite how much I can see Josh isn't sure about her.

"You don't need to bow, I'm not a queen or a royal right now. I'm just a girl from Earth who is lost."

"Then you are mistaken, Adie," Darla says, placing her hand on mine. "This is your home. We have sung songs, shared whispers and carried the rumour of your birth for many years, all in hopes you will come and save us all. The land you stand on needs you; the magic it once held and shared with everyone is long gone. We now have but a fraction of the power that we used to have. Frayan is dying under Queen Lilyanne's rule. It needs you."

"I can't save everyone. I'm sorry, I just can't," I say, shaking my head and stepping back from her as a humourless laugh leaves my lips. "I needed a dragon to save me last time I was in trouble."

"You have much to learn, Adie. Now, let's sit and have a drink," Darla says, and the disappointment is thick in her voice and completely impossible to miss. Josh looks at me, and I shake my head. I know he thinks the same thing. I can't just pretend what they are saying isn't real, because it is. They are real people, who clearly think I'm here to save them, when the truth is, I have no clue how to fight a queen. I have no idea how to fix Frayan, and I don't want to lie to give them false hope that I can help them. Josh sits next to me on the bench, not leaving more than a few inches of space between us. I almost sigh in relief when his hand rests next to mine, and he links a few of his fingers with mine.

"Adie didn't know who she was or anything much about this world until recently," Josh explains to Darla.

"Did your mother, the queen, not tell you?" Darla asks. "Queen Asteria was always very knowledgeable about the world. She spent years travelling until her parents died, and then she took the throne."

"She was imprisoned on Earth, and I was brought up by other parents. I thought I was just a wolf shifter until I found my mother," I explain to her.

"Is she alive? It would be wonder—"

"No, she died in my arms," I whisper, but the words echo around the room.

"I am so sorry for your loss. I must ask, was the

royal power shared?" Darla asks me as she pours the drinks. I wait until she hands me a cup of something that smells sweet and feels warm to hold. I assume she is talking about the power my mother gave me that I never really understood.

"What is the royal power?" I ask.

"The royals had control over their court, the trees, the ground, and the very magic that the court owns. The Autumn court is the only court with a little magic left since the other three courts' magic has been taken by Queen Lilyanne. She wishes for you to give her the royal power, and then she would be the true ruler," Darla says, though she sounds disgusted. "If she took the Autumn power, then this court would die much like the others have."

"I have the power," I tell her, because there is no point in lying.

"Thank the gods," Darla says with pure joy in her eyes as she smiles at me. "The fact you survived the transfer of power gives me hope that one day you will be able to stop Queen Lilyanne. Many heirs have died from not being the rightful ruler and not being able to handle the power."

"So this Lily has the power of three courts?" I ask.

"Yes, but she cannot use them all without harming herself. She is from the Summer court, and that is her only place of true power, though she never travels there and chooses to live in the Spring court," she tells us.

"Why is that?" Josh asks as I take a sip of the drink, which tastes amazing, and I drink more as Josh and Darla talk.

"I am not sure, but I suspect it's because she killed her parents in the Summer court, and it is a place of ghosts for her," she replies. "Or so the rumours say."

"We came to ask you about portals to Earth or Dragca. Are there any?" Josh asks.

"No. The royals sometimes can pull portals open, but only on special days. There was one about ten years ago, but there will not be another for a long time," she says what we both suspected and didn't want to hear. I look to Josh, who drinks from his cup as he looks away, his whole body tense.

"Do you know of a prophecy? One that might make Lilyanne want me dead?" I ask.

"No one knows the words, but yes, there is a prophecy. It was rumoured to be told to Lilyanne on her sixteenth birthday," she explains to me. "It was also rumoured that a fate told it. I'm sorry I don't know more."

"No, you've answered a lot. Thank you for your help," I say, placing my empty cup on the side before standing up. I cross my arms, looking out of the small window in the room which looks over the village. "Do you know anything about my father? Any siblings?" I ask.

"No, you were a blessing to the Autumn queen, but I know little of your father. I know he must have been special to steal our queen's heart," she softly tells me. "Your family were always known as kinder than anyone in Frayan. They were extremely loved, as you would be if people knew you were here."

"No one can know, for Adelaide's safely," Josh is quick to put that idea down.

"Adelaide...that was your grandmother's name. She was said to be a wonderful leader, much like your mother. I can see them both in your soul," Darla says, walking over to me. She places her hands on my shoulders, smiling at me. "I can only speak as a mother who loves her child very much when I say that your family would want you to do whatever you feel is right. We have lived in the shadows of peaceful time for many years. The snow has not fallen on the Winter court in many years, the Spring court sees no more baby animals in the fields, and the Summer court no longer is sunny as it once was. The world will wait for its saviour if that is not you. You must do what is best for you, Adelaide. This is your home, but I see that you are not sure of that yet. I do wish to the fates and gods that you change your mind."

"We should be leaving," Josh sternly says, and Darla lowers her hands.

"Your secret is safe with me, and you will always be the true ruler of Frayan in my eyes," Darla says with thick emotion in her tone. I can only stare at her, wide-eyed as I pull my hood up and follow Josh to the door. He opens it and walks out, and I look back at Darla for a second.

"Thank you for helping us. I will think on what you said. I don't know who I am right now, but I want to find out," I tell her, being as honest as I can. Everything about who I am and Frayan itself feels like it's swallowing me under all the pressure it gives off.

"Good luck, Adelaide," Darla gently says with a supportive nod. I turn and walk out of the building, only to see that Jonas isn't back yet.

"We should go and look for him down at that

market," Josh suggests as he pulls the hood of his cloak up. I link my hand with his, letting him lead me back down the steps and into the market. We walk further down into the cave, where it opens up into a giant circle full of people and more stalls in mini caves.

I see Jonas with Winnie by a stall displaying many herbs, just as a loud noise like a hawk's squawk fills my ears. People start shouting as the noise fades away, and they all rush past us, heading for the entrance. Josh and I have no choice but to walk with the crowd towards the entrance, where the ground is littered with hundreds of little notes. I look up to see a flash of blue light, and then there is nothing but trees and sky. The notes are black, folded in half and cover the ground. People start picking them up as I lean down and grab one, opening it to read what is inside.

"You know who you are, and I know who you love. Rick, Mich and Nath are with me. If you wish to see your three saviours once again, you must come to see me. I await your arrival in the Spring court. Queen Lilyanne, the one true queen of Frayan."

EIGHT

ADELAIDE

"We have to go to get them back," I say, turning around at the door of the cabin and eyeing Josh and Jonas who have been debating what to do since we got here. I look around us, seeing and sensing no one before lowering my hood.

"It could be a trap. There is no way to know if she actually has them," Jonas comments with a long sigh. "Lilyanne could have learnt their names—"

"They would come for Adie, I know it. My pack would follow her anywhere; that was clear from the first day that we met. They are here," Josh interjects into Jonas's voice of reason, and I try not to smile at his words. I'm starting to realise I would follow them anywhere too. As soon as I read the note, I just wanted to leave and go to rescue them, but the guys wanted us to come back to the cabin right away and talk about it in private. I understand why we needed to leave the village. It wasn't safe when everyone was talking about the notes, and we are the new outsiders. I don't even know if we can rescue them from Lily. It's clearly going to be a trap.

"How did those notes get left outside the village in the first place?" I ask. "I heard something like a hawk and saw a flash of light."

"I don't know, but if there is a chance Queen Lilyanne knows where we are, we should leave," Jonas suggests, and Josh is quick to agree. They start talking between each other, coming up with safe places to stay and hide for the night while I pace next to them. I turn and look out at the moon high in the sky. It's unnaturally large, taking up the entire night sky and making it look breathtakingly stunning. The moon makes me want to shift and howl loudly and hear my pack howl with me. But they won't. Not when she has them, and I am not doing anything to get them back.

"I am going to the Spring court to save my pack. Josh, are you coming with me?" I ask Josh first, walking until I'm stood right in front of him and Jonas. Josh smirks at me, placing his hands on his hips and looking rather surprised at my demanding question.

"I am forever at your side, sweetheart, and they are my family too. We will go," Josh replies to me. "You say you don't want to rule and be a queen, but in this moment, you remind me of the woman who brought me up, Queen Winter."

"She does, doesn't she?" Jonas says, rubbing his chin. "A queen to admire. I believe you'd get along well with Queen Isola as well. She was brought up on Earth, you know?"

"I didn't know that. Funny how we all started in the same place, but fate has sent us to three different worlds," I say quietly, though the silence of the forest makes me feel like the trees are listening in to our every word. "I'm not like them, though. They are queens."

"You are an heir, a princess, if you will," Jonas reminds me, and I awkwardly rub my arm before looking away.

"Jonas, I will understand if you don't want to come with us to save my pack," I change the subject to get us back on point, because I honestly can't talk about this right now. My heart isn't focused on Frayan and my personal heritage and past. My heart and soul only want to save my pack right now. If they die, I don't know how I would cope with it.

"I am a trained dragon guard, mainly trained to protect royals, as the Dragca royal family like to keep family closer than strangers. See, I never did fit in with the world of Dragca, I always felt like an outsider. I love my family, but I was always wanting to be on Earth, searching for a purpose to my life. Now, I like Frayan more than Dragca and Earth. Both Dragca and Earth have bad memories for me, shadows and a past that I can never forget when I'm there," he explains to me. I want to ask what happened, but he carries on talking. "That's not the point though. You are a royal, and it would be my honour to be your first formal guard. I will protect you to the best of my abilities and die to keep you alive if you so wish it. My dragon will be yours as will my allegiance. Will you accept?" he asks me, and he lowers himself onto one knee in front of me, bowing his head.

"I'm not a typical royal, Jonas," I nervously say, still rubbing my arm enough to make it sore. I lower my hand and try to keep myself standing tall. This is serious to him; I can feel it.

"Who ever is?" he asks with a smile as he looks up. "From what I've seen so far, I am honoured to protect you. You will be queen, Adelaide. You could say I sense it. Maybe my seer adoptive mother has been rubbing off on me."

"I haven't done anything to deserve your alliance, Jonas," I say, having a feeling I'm not going to be able to say no to him.

"Say yes so he can get up and we can pack. We have shit to do," Josh says in a bored tone, and I grin at him because, for a second, he sounds more like my moody Josh that I've grown to like. There was even a note of playfulness in there.

"I accept," I say with a sigh, and Jonas beams at me as he stands up and swiftly bows his head once more.

"As your guard, I suggest we all go inside until nightfall, then we can make our way to the Spring court. It is about four days' travel on foot," he explains to me. "It's a nice trip and safe enough, as not many people live outside the Spring court from what I've seen."

"Shame we can't fly, as that might give us away," Josh grumbles as Jonas unlocks the cabin, and we all go inside. A pink bundle flies straight into Josh, right past me but leaving a trail of pink dust in her wake.

"Tay, you're awake," I say as Josh looks to the side at Tay, who is sitting on his shoulder with her legs crossed. She raises an eyebrow at me, and I get the feeling she is annoyed with me somehow. Why is the crazy pixie always mad at me?

"The fates are calling us both. You must come with me. Now," she says, though the guys just look confused, and I rub my forehead.

"You can't understand her, can you?" I ask them.

"Since when could you understand her?" Josh asks me.

"More secrets," I mutter, and Josh just takes a deep breath rather than reply to that.

"What is she saying?" Jonas asks, looking curious as he walks up to Tay and looks at her. She flies off Josh's shoulder and goes into the kitchen. We all run after her as she starts opening the dark wooden cabinets. She stops, finding a bowl, and I duck as she throws it at me.

"No throwing!" I shout at her, but of course, she doesn't listen. If anything, she looks more furious. I have the feeling I shouldn't have shouted at her.

"Why are you still here? Go to fates!" she screams back at me, picking up another bowl and throwing it. I jump behind the wall by the door, where Jonas and Josh are hiding.

"This seems like an argument between two women that we shouldn't get involved in," Jonas says as a plate comes flying out the room and smashes onto the floor.

"You two are big babies. She is a tiny pixie!" I glare at them as I speak.

"Yes, but she isn't throwing the stuff at us, so this is your problem," Josh replies, clearly siding with Jonas.

"Oh, for the love of god," I mutter, running past the door and jumping onto the sofa. I hide behind it as Tay flies out, holding a heavy clay plate in her hands and a vindictive look in her eye. She is desperate to hit me with that plate. Before she can throw the plate, I stand up, holding my hands in the air.

"Hit me with that plate, and Rick will be super mad," I warn her. "I will tell him." It's a cheap shot, but she glares at me for all of two seconds before dropping the plate—which smashes to pieces—and flies over to sit on Josh's shoulder.

"Tay, that wasn't nice," Josh says to her. All the

help he is now. "What is wrong anyway? What did she say?" he asks.

"That the fates are calling us, and apparently I have to go with her," I explain to him.

"Fates?" Jonas asks.

"The old gods. Does dragon not know where he came from?" Tay asks in an extremely patronising tone with a glare in Jonas's direction.

"The dragon saved your pixie ass, so why don't you try being nicer?" I say, and she huffs, which makes more glitter sprinkle all over Josh's black cloak.

"I follow you to this world because you are important. We need to go. Have you not heard their call?" she asks.

"No—"

"Liar. You are child of fate. They call to you," she says, crossing her arms, her creepy little pink eyes watching me.

"It doesn't matter right now. Rick, Mich and Nath are in trouble in this world, and we are going to save them. Are you coming with us?" I ask her.

"Rick is threatened?" Tay says, her overly confident composure cracking when I mention Rick. I know, in her own way, she loves him and the rest of our pack.

"Yes, Rick needs us to help him before the queen kills him," I explain to her. She goes to say something when she turns her head to the window, and I hear it as well.

"Come to me, fate wolf. You must heed my call."

"Adie?" Josh gently says my name, snapping me out of it, and I look towards him as Tay starts to speak.

"I care deeply for my family, the ones who saved me, but I cannot resist the call of fate. No one should ignore it. I think you should come with me," she says. "You are important."

"But I have to save Rick, Mich and Nath," I tell her.

"This is a really creepy one-sided conversation," Jonas mutters, and Josh smirks at him for a second.

"You are making mistake. Only the fates can save us all now," she replies, ignoring Josh and Jonas.

"I would make a million mistakes over and

over again if it meant my pack was all alive at the end," I coldly tell her, slightly disappointed that she is choosing to go to some fates over saving Rick.

"You aren't just Frayan royal. When you find out the truth, you will be sad you did not come with me now," she says, before jumping off Josh's shoulder and transforming into an owl. She flies straight through the window, smashing it into pieces before she flies off into the forest.

"I'm guessing the pixie isn't coming with us?" Jonas asks.

"No, she isn't. We are on our own," I say, the words never meaning more than they do right now. I expected my pack to come and save me, take me back to Earth, and I could pretend none of this happened.

I could pretend the whole of Frayan hadn't been waiting for me for years, and I let them down because I'm no saviour.

Now I'm being forced to walk right into a trap to save the men who have become a permanent part of my life.

I have to save my pack.

T run past the trees, leaves brushing against my paws as they float up into the air in my wake, the scents of the forest soothing me. I stop when I've gone too far, when I know Josh and Jonas are going to take a minute to catch up to me. I drop my bag from my mouth onto the ground before sitting back and letting out a long howl. My howl echoes as I shift back into my human form, naked on the cold forest floor. I shiver as I pull my clothes out of the bag, pull them on, and clip my cloak on last.

I'm sliding the bag onto my back just as I hear a sweet song being sung. I pause, looking to my left where I can see a campfire in the distance and the sound of someone singing. I quietly walk through the trees until I can see the small group of people surrounding a campfire. They all have brown cloaks on, and they are watching a woman who is playing a guitar and singing. I hide behind the tree as I listen to her enchanting song, not wanting to interrupt her.

> *"Will you listen to the song of the*
>   *courts?*
> *A song sung of peaceful times, of a*
>   *time of love and joy?*
> *Will you listen to the song I sing?*
> *Let it bless your soul and bring you*
>   *hope.*
> *A hopeful heart of love and pure*
>   *peace.*
> *A distant memory of a time we all*
>   *seek.*
> *A time when snow fell on Winter, and*
>   *the people danced in love.*
> *Will you listen to the song of the*
>   *courts?"*

THE SONG CARRIES ON, but I step away because I know I'm intruding on them, and the more I hear of this peaceful time of the courts, the more I feel guilty that I'm not able to help them. To win a war, I would need an army. I would need loyal supporters and a good grip on my powers. At the moment, all I have is a name, a memory and three of my pack in the enemy's dungeon. They say I'm their saviour, but I'm not. The more I tell myself it, the more I want to believe them and change it. I just don't know how to do that. I wonder what my parents would say. What would they have wanted me to do? Did my mother miss Frayan when they came to Earth?

"You went a little too far ahead. I was getting worried," Josh says as he gets to my side, looking me over to make sure I'm okay. "When you said you wanted to go for a run, I didn't expect you to go so far."

"Sorry, I didn't mean to worry you. My wolf was just overly excited to be free," I explain to him, and he nods as Jonas comes up to us. He doesn't say anything; he just carries on walking, and we follow.

"Did you hear the singing?" I ask Josh as we

head through the trees, where I hear water in the distance.

"No, but then I don't have wolf senses, Adie," he tells me, and I sometimes forget he isn't a wolf. "Do you know much about angels?"

"No, my parents didn't let me learn anything about the other supernaturals," I explain to him.

"Well, there are light and dark angels. You can easily tell them apart by the colour of their wings. Black is dark and white is light. Our powers are opposites as well. Light angels can see glimpses of the future and heal people," he tells me.

"And dark angels, like you?" I ask, because I love his black wings and could never forget them.

"We can cause pain with a single touch and see the past. I could take your hands and show you your birth and everything that happened after it if you want," Josh suggests. I think about it in silence for a while as we get to the river, which is the end of the forest. The river is shallow, filled with white and bright blue stones that reflect off the purple water.

"We should camp here for the night. We have been walking all day, and this is the border to the Spring court where everything is a little more complicated," Jonas explains to me, pointing at the other side of the river, where there are no trees, just a massive open field that stretches further than I can see. The field is full of yellow grass with tiny purple flowers sprinkled all across it. I nod, pulling my bag off and placing it near the trees to give us shelter in case it rains. Not that I've seen it rain here yet, which is another strange thing. I start picking up fallen logs and sticks to make a fire with Jonas while Josh starts unpacking some of the food and drinks.

"Why are there no animals? Isn't it strange?" I say to Jonas, looking in the river and seeing that there are no fish. My wolf spent a long time trying to find anything living. That's why I found those people, because there isn't anything else to smell. "It's strange because there are still scents of creatures around, but they are long gone."

"I wondered that myself. I've not seen any birds, rabbits or deer. There is no animal anywhere, and it's not right," Jonas replies. "Strangely, I hear wolf howls sometimes in the night. Always far away though."

"Where have they all gone?" I ask.

"I asked Darla about that, and she said when the war started, there were hundreds of animals in the world. They would breed in the Spring court and have their children there before travelling around. She believed the war made them all leave and hide, never to come back again," Jonas tells me. I muse over his words, wondering if the animals did all just decide to leave because of the war. It's the strangest thing I've heard, and some part of me feels sad for the children that are growing up in Frayan and never seeing a real animal. What a cold, heartless world that must be for them, especially as the Frayan people seem to love nature. We are quick to make a fire, and Josh cuts up some of the meat Jonas bought at the market for us all.

"I'm going to walk around the area, make sure we are alone," Jonas tells us, getting up and stretching his legs. "If you need me, just shout."

"Okay," I say, smiling tightly at him as I wrap my arms around my knees, watching the fire that Jonas started. Apparently, that power comes from his half witch side, but he didn't get much power from that. He is more dragon by all accounts, ice dragon to be exact. Josh turns the chicken over before sitting back and resting his arm against mine. I move closer, wrapping my arm around his and resting my head on his shoulder. He tenses for a second before he rests his head on top of mine, and we just watch the fire in silence for a while. The soft sounds of the crackling fire fill my ears, and the running water is just peaceful to relax to.

"I don't want you to show me the past. I know I should want to see my biological parents and everything they no doubt went through to save me, but not now. Not yet," I whisper to him, my words soft.

"You have forever to see those memories. I will be here, waiting for when you want to see," he tells me, comforting me, because I know in the future, I will want to see them.

"Can you see your own past?" I ask.

"Yes. I've seen my mother, who was a full dark angel, give birth to me. She gave me to my father, a full demon, and I never saw her again because she died from the labour. My real father had to go back to hell, so he gave me to my mother's brother to bring me up. Lucifer was a dad to me until he died in the war. He told me once, the last time I saw him actually, that my father used what goodness there was left in his soul to give me a chance at life," he explains to me. "My father took my mother's soul to hell with him so they could be together. I don't know if that is even possible, but Lucifer believed it."

"You're good. You know that, right, Josh?" I ask him, feeling him move his head away from mine, and I look up to see him staring at me. He smirks as he slides a hand into my hair, tugging me closer to him.

"I want to be good for you. I *will* be," he tells me.

"You were before you met me, Josh. I think you just didn't know it," I whisper back to him, and before he can disagree like I know the stubborn man will, I lean up and kiss him. His lips softly press against mine as he pulls me onto his lap, my legs sliding around him as he deepens the kiss. He presses me against his body, kissing me hard enough that I never want this to stop.

In moments like this, I can just pretend it's only me and Josh. That the world isn't falling apart around us, and we don't have to save it.

I can pretend I'm not falling in love with another man in my pack, hopelessly knowing this is going to cause problems.

CHAPTER
TEN
ADELAIDE

"Welcome to the Spring court, aka the busiest court in the whole of Frayan," Jonas says as we come up over a large hill and stand at the top, looking down at the massive city below. The centre of the city is a clear dome, which looks like one large piece of crystal has been dropped from the sky, and it now makes the centrepiece of the city. Hundreds of houses in circles surround the crystal, stretching out until they stop at large stone walls. The stone walls completely surround the city, and they are tall enough to cast a long shadow into the fields around it. Inside the dome, there are a lot of plants and trees by the looks of it. There is also a castle, and I'm taking a wild guess that I will find

Lily and my pack in there. There is something up the side of the dome, possibly steps, and a stage at the top. A stage for a queen no doubt.

"It might be busy, but it is also very beautiful," I say, because beautiful is a big understatement to how lovely this place truly is. I think it's how the light reflects off the dome that makes it shinier and more stunning to look at.

"I have a plan," Josh proudly states.

"Like a plan that is going to get us in there, you know, unseen?" Jonas asks, crossing his arms and raising his eyebrow at Josh. Four days walking here, listening to these two wind each other up, is enough to make any woman lose her mind. I swear I'm inches away from it. They are both having a seriously annoying bromance.

"Well, Rick has an obsession with these wizard films that the humans made. In the movie, they use potions to dress—" Josh starts to explain, but I've watched those films.

"To get in the building. I've watched Harry Potter. But we don't have that kind of potion here," I say, confused.

"But they must have guards. If we can knock out a few guards, we could dress up as them and get inside, no problem," he says. Ah, I get him. I've seen that done in a few movies actually, but this isn't a movie. We could easily be caught, especially when Lily is actively looking for us. I guess I don't have any other plan of getting in there though.

"Who knew Harry Potter logic would be saving our asses?" Jonas says with a grin.

"Rick will love this when he finds out," Josh mutters, rubbing his face before looking at me and Jonas as we chuckle.

"What if, no matter what we do, we are walking into a trap?" Jonas is quick to point out. "It's clear she wants you dead, Adie. Maybe you should stay here while Josh and I go to get the others."

"That isn't happening. We should stay together, and you will need my help," I say. I might be the only reason Lily doesn't kill Josh and Jonas if she captures them. I have to be there.

"Adie, Jonas has a point," Josh says.

"If she catches you both and assumes I'm not coming for the others, she will kill you all. I saw it in her eyes, she is mad. A mad queen who will do nothing but destroy the world to make sure she gets what she wants. I know I have to go with you," I firmly say.

"For the record, I think this is a bad idea,"

Jonas says, shaking his head before he starts walking down the hill.

"If she hurts you, I will find a way to make sure she dies," Josh states, and I don't doubt him. I take his hand, almost to reassure him as best I can, before we start walking towards the Spring court. The walk is mostly silent, and I make sure to keep my hood up the moment we get near the walls. There are large white crystal archways in the walls, where people are walking in and out. There are three guards on each side of the archway, and I know we can't grab any of those guards, because they are too out in the open.

We join a crowd of light blue haired teenagers who are carrying big bags of folded clothing down the pathway into the main part of the city. I keep my head down, as do Jonas and Josh, just in case anyone looks our way. They don't though, and we easily walk straight into the city and through the streets of the village. The streets are lined with wooden and stone houses, and each one has a crystal symbol of a dove on the door. The crystal doves are hanging all over the place, and they are hard to miss as the sunlight catches them.

"I know the best place to find guards off duty," Jonas proudly states.

"Where?" I ask Jonas, following his gaze to a sign hanging above the door of a bigger house than the others.

The Spring Court Pub.

"You were right about there being guards here...just a little too right," I say as we sit down at an empty table, eyeing all the many, many guards in here drinking. There must be a good twenty guards who are flirting with the waitresses with blonde, streaked purple hair and not much clothing. I roll my eyes when one of those women spots us and drifts her eyes over Jonas and Josh. Josh protectively wraps an arm around the back of my chair as the woman comes over, sitting on the edge of the table. I keep my hood up, covering my face and hair, but Jonas and Josh have removed theirs.

"Now what can I get you to drink, my handsome strangers?" she asks.

"What court are you from?" Jonas asks her instead.

"Doesn't my hair give it away, handsome?" she

asks with a flirty laugh, and Jonas smirks. "Or are you teasing me a little?"

"Blue is for Winter, red is for Autumn, and orange is for Summer...so that makes you a Spring Fray," Jonas says, and the waitress only laughs.

"Of course! Do you want a room to sleep in tonight? I waitress here in the day, and at night, I bartend at the inn next door," she explains. "I could gladly have a word and get you a big room."

"We will have three drinks of whatever you would suggest after a long travel from the Autumn court. I will think about the room," Jonas softly says.

"Coming right up, big man," she says, sliding off the table and kissing Jonas on the cheek before giggling and running away.

"Someone likes you," I point out.

"My dragon wants to freeze her to the floor," Jonas sarcastically grumbles. "My hands have frozen the tops of my trousers in an attempt to keep my dragon under control."

"So your dragon chooses who you like?" I ask, curious. My wolf doesn't have that control over me in any regard, though she does trust some people and hate others.

"I trust my dragon more than I trust myself at times, and most dragon shifters feel the same. We know that our dragon is always going to choose a mate who they know will be our equal. They won't take less than that," he explains to me. "Sometimes I believe my dragon is far more intelligent than I am."

"That's almost romantic," I say, and Josh's hand slides onto my shoulder.

"What did I say about the flirting, J?" Josh says, and Jonas smirks as he leans back in his seat.

"I can't help it if every word I say your girl-friend finds romantic," he replies, and I grin, trying not to laugh, and as Josh and Jonas continue to argue, I see the door on the side open and shut. I read the sign on the door, which says Steam Room, and smile to myself. The guys don't even notice as I get up and go to the door, pushing it open and seeing the piles of guard uniforms on the bench, and the steam room behind it. I go back to the table just as the waitress comes back with our drinks and places them on the table. This time she sits on Jonas's lap and starts playing with his hair as she giggles, and he looks incredibly uncomfortable. Poor dragon.

"I found a way to solve our problem," I whisper to Josh. "Want to use the steam room and perhaps get our clothes mixed up with the guards'?"

"I think that sounds like a perfect idea, sweetheart," he whispers back and leans in to kiss me. As we kiss, I start to realise we might have another problem when we do get Rick, Nath and Mich out of the castle. What if Josh wants me just for himself?

ELEVEN

ADELAIDE

"It's unfair how well this uniform fits you two, and me? I look ridiculous," I mutter as my nerves have taken over now that we are walking up the dome. I'm just word vomiting random stuff now, hoping that if I keep talking, it will make this place and what we are doing seem less terrifying. Josh and Jonas are walking a little in front of me, keeping me as much out of view as possible, because they fit in well, looking the part of a normal guard. The uniform keeps slipping off my shoulder, and the helmet smells terrible as well as being huge. In the end though, nothing matters except for two things: getting our pack back and somehow escaping here alive. Those are the important things and the ones I am the most nervous about.

"We shouldn't talk. It will give us away," Jonas says, and I know he is right, so I keep my thoughts to myself as we get to the entrance of the dome. It is huge, stretching so high in the sky that I can't see the top of it anymore. There is only one entrance by the looks of it, and it is guarded well. We walk up to the archway, and to our surprise, one of the guards simply moves to the side and lets us through. I don't need to look at Josh or Jonas to know that was weird. They should have asked why we are coming this way, and we had an excuse all planned out.

I look around after entering, and I was right about what was inside the dome. It's a beautiful castle right in the middle of what I can only describe as a rain forest. Tall, purple trees line a pathway to the castle, and flowers as tall as the trees grow around them. The grass is almost orange in colour, and the bushes dotted around with more flowers are many different colours. It's honestly stunning. Every one of our footsteps against the stoned path seems so much louder in the silence as we head to the castle only to find another row of guards. This time they don't move as we stand in front of them.

"The queen ordered us to come to her," Josh says in a commanding tone.

"The queen commanded us to capture and contain anyone who attempts to come in here," the guard in the middle says, pulling out his sword, and his friends do exactly the same.

"The hard way it is, then," Jonas grumbles and then blasts ice into the chests of two of the guards who go flying into the air. Josh is quick to spread his wings out and grab me around the waist. A scream leaves my lips at the same time my feet leave the ground, and he zooms us up into the dome. I wrap my arms and legs tightly around him, closing my eyes in fear before I feel him land and then I can open them again. We are stood on the stone balcony in the middle of the castle, and I breathe in deeply as I slide off Josh.

"Was that planned?" I ask him.

"Yeah, Jonas suggested it when you slept last night," he explains to me. "A backup plan if trouble comes up. Anyway, he is handling himself fine," Josh says, waving a hand at Jonas, who is fighting the guards off and looking like he is enjoying himself as he does. Josh goes to turn the handle of the door when it is slammed open, knocking him back. As Queen Lilyanne steps out, Josh moves in front of me and pulls out his sword.

"Bring him," Lily says, her voice loud enough to echo in the room behind her. Seconds later, Nath walks out to Lily's side, with a guard right behind him, holding a dagger to his neck. Nath's once dirty blond hair now has light blue tips and streaks of blue throughout it, almost like highlights. Being in Frayan must have done this. His hands are tied behind his back, his clothes are ripped in places, and he looks tired and dirty, yet all I want to do is hug him. My heart beats loudly in my ears as Lily pulls out a dagger from her long red dress and carelessly presses it against Nath's heart.

"Adie, I'm sorry. Go—" Nath starts to say, but Lily interrupts him.

"Little Nath here is one of my subjects, though a half breed bastard, is he not?" she says, and I grit my teeth.

"Let him go," I growl, stepping to Josh's side, despite how he tenses, and I know he wanted me to stay behind him.

"I am queen here. Not you. You do not give the orders, do you understand?" she shouts, and I cry out as she cuts a deep line into Nath's chest, letting blood pour down his grey shirt. He doesn't make a noise, though I can see the pain in his expression. I can almost feel it, and I quickly lose control. My arms start buzzing with electricity as two lines of pain scratch down my back, and I turn my gaze to see glowing blue wings floating behind me.

"You are a mad queen," I spit out. "Now let him go."

"I'm going to make this simple for you, child. You put these on..." She slides out a simple pair of silver handcuffs, but when I look closer, it looks like diamonds are impressed into the metal. "And play nice, or I will kill this sweet lover of yours. Then your demon friend and everyone else you care about next. You say I'm mad, but I am also honest. I promise this will be the fate of your lovers if you do not put these on." She throws them onto the ground at my feet. Every part of my body resists me as I pick up the handcuffs off the ground. A Fray promise is unbreakable. I remember the seer warning me of that, and I wonder if she saw my fate all along.

"Don't—" Josh whispers, but I know there isn't another choice. I clip the handcuffs on, gasping as they burn into my skin for a second and carry on stinging. My wings disappear behind me, and my power feels completely gone. I can't even sense my wolf anymore.

"I did what you asked. Let them go," I whimper.

"I promised no such thing, little child. Throw them in the dungeons; I will deal with them tomorrow," Lily says, her lips pulled up into a victorious smile. She may have won this battle, but the fight is not over yet.

More guards flood into the balcony, and two grab Josh, making him follow the ones holding Nath out of the doors. I don't bother resisting the guards as they roughly grab my arms and start dragging me through a corridor and down three flights of stone stairs. I trip a few times, but luckily, they are gripping me so tightly that I can't fall. At the end of the staircase is a heavy wooden door with metal arrows on it. The guard holding Nath unlocks the door, but Nath's eyes are on me as he is pulled into the room. Josh is dragged in next, and I'm pushed in last, tumbling into Josh's arms as the door is pulled shut behind us and locked.

"Nath, you back?" I hear Rick say, sounding like he just woke up. Dozens of lights shaped like tiny spheres fill the room, and I turn to see Rick and Mich sitting on the floor on the other side of the room, Mich's hand in the air, making the spheres appear. I don't wait for Rick to say anything, and neither does he, as we run to each other. I throw my arms around his shoulders, pressing myself as tightly as I can to him as he holds me back just the same.

"Adelaide," he murmurs into my ear, and I sigh from the emotions running through me.

"I missed you," I tell him, pulling back to smile. "All of you."

"We missed you too, could you not tell? We came to save you, but that doesn't look like it worked."

"It's okay," I say, wrapping my arms around him. Mich and Josh carefully lower Nath to the ground just as the door is opened and Jonas comes tumbling into the room.

"Assholes!" Jonas shouts and looks around at us. "I guess we fell for the trap."

"Jonas?" Rick questions as I let him go and lean down in front of Nath, taking his hand.

"You okay?"

"I will live. I'm sorry we are in a big mess," Nath says, and I shake my head. The lights flicker a few times, and I look to Mich, who is struggling and looking tired.

"I can't hold the lights for much longer. This place drains my magic like a vacuum," Mich explains.

"Adie, come close," Nath says, and he whispers to me as I rest at his side. "I know the dark scares you, but we will all be here." I can't believe he remembered that from our date.

"Where is Tay? In fact, why don't you tell me everything that happened since you got here. It looks like we have some waiting to do," Rick asks, coming to sit at my side. Josh and Mich rest against the wall on either side of Nath, and Jonas comes to sit on my left. I rest my head on Rick's shoulder as the lights fade out, and I start telling the story of how we have survived in Frayan so far.

They might be the only ones I ever tell it to if we don't get out of this mess.

TWELVE

"Josh, mate, could you sit down? All the pacing is freaking me out," Mich grumbles as I lift my head from Rick's shoulder, wiping my sleepy eyes as I wake up. There are no windows in here, so I have no idea how long we have been locked up down here, but we all suspect it's been at least a good twelve hours. I don't know what Lily is waiting for. If she wants me dead, why is she messing around and waiting? Rick, Nath and Mich have long given up trying to find a way to escape this place and have come to the conclusion that we can't just get out. It must be magically locked somehow, because no one can shift or use their powers.

I rub my wrists as Josh sits down, and I see

him glaring at Mich in the corner of my eye. The bracelets are so tight, but they aren't stinging anymore, which is at least one good thing. It doesn't stop the panic over how I can't feel my wolf and how disconnected I feel from myself. Mich has a ball of dim light floating in the middle of the room, but he can only hold it for a tiny amount of time without hurting himself. Whatever this room is lined with affects Jonas too, and he can't connect to his dragon without a lot of pain, which we soon learnt made him pass out. Rick said the same thing happened to them when they tried to shift.

Even though Nath is injured, Lily hasn't hurt any of them before him. I just don't understand her, and I have a feeling I need to have some idea of who she is in order to escape this.

"How is the cut?" I ask Nath, picking myself up off the ground and walking over to him. He doesn't stop me as I pull his shirt to the side a little, seeing the long cut that isn't healing as it should be. It looks almost blue, like it's kissed with frost from a cold day or something. I place my hand on his cheek, seeing his dazed eyes and how tired he is.

"Nath doesn't look right," I say to the others, and Nath takes my hand, linking our fingers.

The room suddenly feels a little more tense for the simple action and how none of us have talked about any of this. I look back to see both Rick and Josh staring at our linked fingers, and it takes them a second to snap out of it. Mich comes right over to us first, placing his hand on Nath's forehead before leaning back.

"How do you feel?" Mich asks, tilting his head to the side and meeting my eyes for a moment. He is good at hiding his emotions, but I see it. He is concerned. There aren't healers here, and so far, I haven't seen a hospital in Frayan. I don't even know how they heal people here. I feel nothing but powerless as I stare at Nath.

"Like shit. I should have healed by now," Nath admits, thankfully not hiding the situation from us.

"It's this magic room; it's affecting all our powers, including healing. I imagine Lily likes to use this room to let her victims slowly die," I point out and cringe when Nath humourlessly laughs and shakes his head.

"You are certainly making me feel better, Adie, love," Nath jokes, and I give him a sympathetic smile just as I hear the door being pushed open. Three guards walk into the room, their black uniforms covering all of them, the jewels reflecting off the fire on the wall outside the room. The one in the middle looks straight at me as he comes a little further into the room. Though he is looking at me, his eyes constantly flicker to everyone, watching for the slightest chance of danger.

"The girl comes with us. Cause trouble, and we will kill one of you. The queen orders it so," the guard simply says, pulling out his sword and daring us to cause trouble.

"Adie isn't fucking going—" Rick starts to say, coming to my side, and I place my hand on his chest, stopping him.

"Don't, Rick. I will be okay," I say, pressing my hand harder into Rick's chest, trying to calm him down when he looks like he wants to burn the entire world down rather than let me out of his sight. He looks down at me as the others gather around, and I know they all want to fight their way out of this to save me. I just can't let them die for me. "Pack is family. Family trusts each other. Trust me, please?" He finally nods, and I can breathe again.

"If you harm her, I will find a way out of here,

and I will be coming for you first," Josh warns the guard.

"Understood," the guard replies, and I don't think any of us expected him to reply to us.

"Do you know who she is?" Nath asks from where he is sitting.

"A prisoner for our queen," the guard replies, turning his head to eye Nath.

"She is Adelaide Autumn, heir to the Autumn court. The world you stand on is changing, and trust me, you don't want to be on Lily's side when the war is over," Nath warns him, making me seem like something so much more than I am. I'm an heir to a fallen court, to dead parents and a world I don't know. I'm an outsider...how am I meant to take a throne?

"We serve the queen," the guard firmly says, though I don't actually believe him. I sense he is lying. Even though my powers are blocked, I still have some of my senses, it seems.

"Which queen? The way I see it, there are two royals. One is crazy and killing your world. The other is amazing; she just needs a chance to prove it," Nath says, and his words make me smile. He really does believe in me.

"Even if I could help you, my family would suffer. The royal guard has no choice but to do what we are told. I am sorry, princess Adelaide," the guard tells me. "Now we must leave."

"I understand," I whisper, because there is nothing I wouldn't do for my family.

"Be careful," Josh says, lifting my other hand and gently kissing the tips of my fingers before letting me go. Rick, Mich and Nath don't say anything, but they don't have to. They don't like me going without them, but what choice do we really have right now? I turn around and walk to the guard, who turns and walks up the stairs, with me having no choice but to follow.

The guards lock the door behind us before following close behind me, their presence making me more than nervous. We climb two sets of stairs before the guard opens a door and holds it for me to enter a long hallway. The hallway has stone walls and dark wooden floor panels that creak as we walk across them. There are no paintings or anything on the walls, but I notice there are hooks where something was hung up before. The guard stops before a door, knocking it two times before opening it and walking in. I step into the room, which is a study for all accounts, and sitting behind a desk is Lily. She has her arms crossed as she leans back in the strangely old, almost broken wooden chair. Surely a royal would have a padded chair around to sit on?

"Leave us alone," Lily commands, and the guards are quick to leave the room, shutting the door as Lily stands up, smoothing down her black dress. This one is just as revealing as all the others, cut in places around her stomach to show off her marks. This dress has a high collar, making her look more impressive with the black crown sitting on her head.

"Sit down," she commands, waving a hand at the two seats in front of the fireplace. She goes and sits in the one on the right, crossing her legs and waiting for me. I don't move, knowing I don't want to sit down and talk to her like this is a normal thing. "Sit, or I will behead one of your lovers." I grit my teeth, walking over to the spare seat and sitting down, trying to ignore how comfy the cushioned seat is compared to sitting on the stone floors of the dungeon.

"What do you want?" I ask her.

"When I was eight years old, I made the

mistake of asking my parents why I was so feared —not only by them but by everyone in the courts. Every royal visit, the royals would look at me like I was a monster they wished they could kill," she tells me, throwing me off my track of being neutral to her. "My parents promised they only told me about the prophecy, but I know they lied."

"What else did your parents tell you?" I ask, playing into this little game she has started. I don't understand what she plans to get out of it, but it might help me somehow to understand Lily.

"That a prophecy was spoken, and it was about you and me. I was the bad person, the one everyone feared in this prophecy. So everyone feared what I would become before I even had a chance to make my own choice. The people of Frayan believe fate is your only choice. Many Fray had wanted to kill me as a child, but as a royal child, I was protected at least," she replies to me, picking up a drink off a small table at her side. I stay silent as she sips the red liquid that is too thick to be wine. I actually have no interest in knowing what it is. I know the point of this little story is to make me feel sorry for her, and in some ways, I do. People should not have judged a child so quickly, but she has done terrible things on her own, so now they are right. I watched her expressions, the way she held her body, as she hurt Nath yesterday. She likes the pain in someone's eyes. Thrives off it, I suspect.

"Will you tell me the prophecy?" I ask, because it is the start of all this. I need to know it.

"I hate to repeat it. The prophecy I was told at sixteen is nothing but lies and pain. It set the course for my entire life, and it will do the same for you. Though I will make an allowance for you, Adelaide. Just this once, I will help you," she says, making it sound like she giving me a great honour.

"When the snow stops falling on the
Winter court,
When the sun stops shining high
above the Summer court,
When no creatures are born in the
lands of the Spring court,
A storm will arise and destroy
them all.
The Autumn court heir will return,
bringing death as her shadow.

The Autumn court will rule, the
Autumn court will prevail.
And all who are against her will fall.

On a stormy night, a queen will be
born to the Summer court.
Death will be her tool. Life will be her
ruin.
The heir of Summer and Autumn are
forever linked
by far more than their births alone.
For one cannot live without the other
dying at their hand.

There can only be one queen of the
Frayan courts..."

I RUN the prophecy words over and over in my mind, trying to make sense of it all. The part that stands out the most is the Autumn court heir reference and how there can only be one queen of the Frayan courts. *It can't be Lily.*

"You killed your parents and took over all of Frayan because of some prophecy? What if it isn't real? What if this was *all* for nothing?!" I shout at her, standing up and walking to stand over her. "How many people have you killed for this prophecy? How many lives have you destroyed? The prophecy didn't make you a monster; your own choices did that all on your own!"

"The prophecy made me who I am. I am queen, and no one is here to challenge me!" she says, standing up and glaring at me. We are nearly the exact same height, which means neither of us has to look down as we make our point.

"I never wanted to save Frayan, I only wanted to go home...until now. If I don't stop you, no one ever will. You won't stop. You are a mad queen who wants nothing more than to destroy the entire world!" I say, and she grabs my chin, squeezing tightly. I grip her wrist as she leans closer.

"How do you plan on stopping me when you will be dead tomorrow?" she says, laughing as she lets me go, and I stumble back. Lily walks to the balcony, pushing the doors open and looking back at me. "Come with me, and don't try anything stupid. I will only kill your lovers if you do, and that would be a shame, they are so handsome."

"They are mine," I growl, my throat vibrating

with the warning as I struggle to control my anger. Not that it matters all that much, I can't sense my wolf or any power I could have.

"It's your last night. We should try to at least get along," she says before walking off, and I know there is no point fighting her on this. She is crazy, and this crazy train apparently needs to play out. I walk out onto the balcony, seeing her walking to the edge, where she slowly whistles. When I come to her side, wondering if I just push her over the edge, would she die and this could be all over? A squawk erupts, loud enough to make my ears burn, as something flies up off the ground, and I follow the shadow as it flies around the castle. It heads straight down to us, and I grip the balcony tightly as a bird the size of a horse lands on the balcony, right at Lily's side. She smiles as she places her hand on the bird, which has bright orange feathers and a purple beak. I would say it's a hawk, but I'm not too sure. It doesn't look like any bird I've ever seen. Its eyes watch me so closely, tracking my every breath and movement, I suspect. I'm honestly more scared of this creature than I am of Lily.

"This is Zeno, and he is the last of a great line of birds called Zenilos. When I turned five and received my powers, it soon became clear I would not be gifted with wings. My parents ordered a Zenilo egg to be taken from a nest and given to me. It's a shame the parents had to be killed because they wouldn't let him go. Zeno is my child, the only child I have been blessed with due to the old gods' and fates' cruel ways," she explains to me, affectionately looking at Zeno. "I love him, and he loves me."

"He dropped the notes in front of the village," I say, figuring that out but not how I didn't see him outside.

"Zenilos are special birds for one particular reason. They can teleport themselves wherever they need to go. It makes travel around the courts much easier," she explains to me, placing her hand on Zeno's wing. That's what the burst of light was then.

"I imagine it does," I tightly say. "Why are you showing him to me?"

"I want you to understand I am not completely evil. I am the victim in this world, and I have worked hard to make Frayan a better place. I want you to understand why I must kill you tomorrow," she casually tells me.

"*You* are destroying Frayan," I tell her, but she

only smiles at me before turning her head to look out of the dome.

"See that?" she asks, pointing up high at the top of the dome. From here, I can see a lit up staircase that goes up the side of the dome, and a platform at the top. "I killed your father on top of this dome, with your mother having no choice but to use your father's death as a distraction to escape. I have killed every single royal Frayan on top of this dome, for the whole of Frayan to see. Tomorrow, you will be the last death on this dome. Your lovers will go first. When I die, so will everything Frayan has ever held dear. The royals will be gone, the world will be lost, and my revenge will be complete." She laughs like it is some kind of stupid joke, and I realise something so very important.

"When the snow stops falling on the Winter court, when the sun stops shining high above the Summer court, when no creatures are born in the lands of the Spring court, you have destroyed Frayan. It needs a new queen, a new ruler, and if you touch one of my pack, you will not be on the throne for long." I don't know where those words come from as I say them, but I feel them deep down within my soul, projecting the anger and pain I feel. "A big storm is coming, Queen

Lilyanne, and nothing you do will be able to stop it. You won't be able to stop me."

"Take her away!" Lily screams, and guards rush out the doors. All I hear is Zeno's long squawk as I'm taken away.

THIRTEEN

The cold wind whips against my body as I walk up the crystal steps of the dome, each step dooming my own fate more and more. I've known since the moment the guards came into the prison this morning, forcing all six of us to drink a concoction that would guarantee our powers don't work. Rick looks back at me, his brown eyes locking with mine as we both try not to freak out and let Lily win. We are all being led to our deaths, and I don't see a way out of this for us. I want to tell Rick I think he is my mate too, and it's not just him that feels the connection. I want to tell him a million different things, and yet I'm silent; only the sound of our footsteps and the harsh wind fills our ears. I look behind me for just a second to see Mich, Josh, Jonas and finally Nath walking behind the guard at my back, though Nath is struggling to make it, and the guards are dragging him. It hurts to see him like this, and all I want to do is save him.

Problem is, I can't even save myself.

The guard holds the tip of his sword so that it's just pressing into my lower back every time I move, and it's a reminder to the guys and me that I'd be dead before they could do anything. At this point, I'm going to be dead either way. I might as well jump off these steps and slide down the dome, praying for death. At least Lily wouldn't get to kill me in the same place she killed my father. My hands start to shake with the fear that is coursing through me as we get to the top of the dome and look over at the platform up here. It's very simple; six nooses hang from a metal stand, blowing in the wind. Lily grins as she stands at the side of the platform, looking like she has won this war. She is dressed in black, her long cloak whipping around her body, and her crown standing so high on her head. Imposing. Terrifying. And she wears the worst thing of all—a look of victory.

"Look at the view, not her. Don't give her what she wants to see," Josh says as he walks around the guard, who tries to shove him back, but he doesn't budge. "Look at Frayan, your home." I try to ignore the tears falling down my cheeks as I do what Josh tells me, knowing he wants me to be strong in these last moments. My hands shake so hard that the rest of my body just feels frozen in comparison.

I can smell the city, the thousands of Fray who will be watching this. None of us have had enough time with each other, and everything has been taken from us before we ever got a chance to live it. *I want to live.* I want to fight for Frayan, because everyone is right...it's my home. I look across the meadows and fields, the large mountain in the far distance, which I think is the middle of the island. I can see the courts here, the lines of the river that divide them into four parts. Winter is just behind the mountain, where the ice is so clear that it looks like a rocky river. Spring is where we stand, and behind Autumn must be Summer, the beaches I can just about see. As we are led to the steps up to the block, the guards make us line up before roughly sliding the rope over our necks.

"One way or another, you will die for this. You will never be the queen of Frayan for long," Josh warns her. If we make it out of this, I vow to make sure his words come true. Her cheeks almost go red for a moment in her pure anger, but she quickly smooths her expression, tightening her hands into fists as she moves her eyes to me.

"We all know who has won," she simply says, and I turn my gaze away from her to meet Rick's once more. I need to look at him. If I'm going to die, at least it will be surrounded by my pack. I just wish they weren't dying with me. I wish I could save them.

"I never told you...but I love you, Adelaide. I feel like I've searched for you my entire life, and every part of my fate was to find you and save you. I've failed that...but loving you? It's worth dying for," Rick firmly tells me, his words travelling in the wind for everyone to hear.

"I—" My sentence disappears from my lips as the dome shakes just before smoke, lots of thick black smoke, completely covers us and everything around us. I cough on it, reaching around me to touch Rick. I didn't see where it came from, but I hear the sound of running around us while Lily shouts for us to be killed. I pull the rope off my neck and look behind me as I jump off the platform. Rick and the others follow, reaching for me as they cover their mouths, and I do the same, still coughing on the thick smoke. A gush of wind blows some of the smoke away so I can see all the guards are passed out on the ground, and a shadow of a person is standing over them. She runs to me, offering me a rag to cover my face with. I happily take it as she speaks.

"Unless you all wish to die, we must leave," the woman says, though I can't see her through her cloak. I look to Rick, who nods, and I know this is the best chance we have got. Rick grabs my hand as we all run with her, straight across the dome I can see under my feet until we hit the edge where there is less smoke. The dome brightly reflects the sun, looking shiny and so very steep.

"Where now?" Josh asks, spreading his wings out. "I can take Adie, but not everyone."

"I can take a few, but my dragon isn't listening to me right now," Jonas says, and he must mean the drinks they forced us to swallow this morning, which are no doubt keeping the guys weaker than they are.

"Just jump. You must trust me," the woman states, unclipping a black sphere on her belt, and she chucks it behind us. It smashes, and more black smoke floods out of it, hiding us from anyone's view. The woman walks right to the edge, looking down.

"We don't know you," I say, still coughing on the smoke. She turns to look back at me, not saying a word before jumping off the dome. I guess she wants us to make our own mind up.

"Adelaide! I will find you!" I hear Lily scream, her voice frantic and way too close for my liking. Before the guys can stop me, I let go of Rick's hand and jump off the dome. A scream escapes my lips as I slide down the dome, banging into the side once and crying out when I hurt my shoulder as it slams into the side. I suddenly land on something soft and springy. I bounce and roll down what feels like a hill before I open my eyes and breathe out in relief.

The hooded woman offers me a hand, pulling me up to stand as I breathlessly stare at the giant butterfly we have landed on. It's camouflaged to look like the brown slate roofs of the houses, and you wouldn't know unless you were close that it's a living creature, the camouflage is that good. I think it's a butterfly...but a giant one, the size of three houses.

"Sit behind me. We have to leave before her bird wakes up from the sleeping plant I mixed in his food this morning," the woman tells me, and I might not know her or what she looks like, but I sit down as Josh lands behind me and shakes his head at my decision to jump. Rick, Nath, Mich and Jonas are not far behind, all landing on the butterfly's body after rolling down the wings.

"Sit down quickly," I tell them, and they all form a line behind me as the woman leans down, whispering something to the butterfly I can't hear. I lean back into Josh's arms as the butterfly flaps its wings and is quickly flying us up into the sky, fast enough to make me duck my head down against the wind. When the butterfly starts to glide, I open my eyes and watch the impossible happen. The wings slowly fade from the brown colour they were into a pearly white, mixing with the clouds as we head into them. The body of the butterfly changes to white too, and I look forward to see the eyes of the butterfly are large and pearly white like the wings. Large antennae hover in the air as the creature flies, guiding her way.

"Welcome to Frayan, Adelaide Autumn, heir to the Autumn court. I'm sorry we didn't find you quicker," the woman says as the wind blows back her cloak, revealing light blue hair that looks like frost, and pale skin almost the same colour as snow. She looks back at me with her bright blue eyes shining and a big smile on her lips.

"Thank you. And we?" I ask, wondering if she isn't alone.

"I'm part of the rebellion set up by your mother before you were even born. The rebellion for the true queen of Frayan: you."

FOURTEEN

"We are leaving Frayan," I shout to Josh, watching as we leave the edge of the Autumn court treeline and head straight down the cliff towards the glittering sea. The butterfly glides across the purple sea, and I look down to see a collapsed bridge deep under the water, its silver stone looking like crystals. It's cracked in many places, but still very beautiful. The butterfly directly follows the fallen bridge until we come to an island, with ruins of a castle hanging over the edge of the cliff of the small island. There are no beaches on this side of the island, at least none I can see. The butterfly swerves to the side, around the cliff before making a sharp left into the cliff, where there is an opening, the swerve making a gush of air that forces me to keep my head down. I open my eyes as we fly into a clearing with gaps on either side, and the butterfly lands on the stone, spreading its wings out and making a soothing humming noise.

"Thank you, Nova. You saved us all," the woman says to the butterfly, stroking her back in a loving way. I look back at my pack and Jonas, who all are a little more than tense, watching the woman like she is going to turn around and stab us.

"Welcome to the old Frayan Academy, home of the rebellion, Adelaide," the woman says as she slides down the butterfly's wing and lands smoothly on the ground. Josh spreads his wings out, keeping an arm tightly around my waist as he flies us off the butterfly to land on the ground near the woman.

"Thank you for saving us. We owe you a debt," I say honestly, because we all would be dead if it wasn't for her. "What's your name?"

"Casella, royal heir to the Winter court," she says, offering me a hand to shake, and I gladly accept it. "Seems like you, me and Lilyanne are the only royals left in Frayan. I don't know about you, but I have a feeling we have the same enemy."

"We do. I'm glad to have a new friend. This is Rick, Mich, Nath and Josh—" I start introducing everyone, waving a hand at them, but Jonas clearly wants to introduce himself.

"My name is Jonas LaDrac, and I am from Dragca," he says, bowing his head and then lifting it. They awkwardly stare at each other for a long time, and I raise my eyebrows at Rick who grins at Jonas. The guys all grin at each other, clearly talking in their heads about some kind of joke.

"Dragons. Interesting. The portals have not opened between our worlds in a long time. Are your people still at war? Ice dragons and fire dragons killing each other because they are different?" she asks, crossing her arms and seeming quite defensive. "If they are, you should be back at home fighting for them. This is not your world, Jonas LaDrac."

"The war is ended, and we have a queen called Isola. She would never let a war destroy everything again. One day her child will rule after her," Jonas states, crossing his own arms and looking pretty offended. "As for which world I fight for and what queen, that is my choice. You may not like me here, little Winter princess, but I am staying."

"I'm glad to know Dragca is at peace, and I

never said I didn't want you here, dragon," she replies and looks away from Jonas to me then my pack. "I've heard rumours of Earth having a queen who has fixed a lot of problems," she says, looking expectantly.

"Queen Winter does try her best. The humans are not completely on our side yet," Rick interjects, and there is an awkward silence between us all as I look at Casella, who has turned her gaze to Nath.

"You are from my court, the Winter court," she states, looking at his hair more than anything else. I still feel a pang of jealousy that I don't know where he comes from.

"My father was said to be a guard for the Winter court," Nath explains. "I know nothing else."

"Maybe we can find more information during your time here. The Winter court royal guards weren't a massive group due to my parents not wanting a massive guard in their home. They liked to fight for themselves," Casella explains, and Nath nods, looking away. I'm not sure how much of him wants to find his father. "I will say we are proud people and good fighters. You should be proud to be from the Winter court."

"I thought Lilyanne killed all the royals," Jonas

says, stepping near us and eyeing Casella with caution. Thankfully it takes the heat off Nath, who looks more than a little guarded. "Why did she let you live?"

"Lilyanne doesn't know of my existence, that is why. Asteria and my own mother worked together, knowing that Lilyanne was going to destroy all the courts. My father and Adelaide's believed she wouldn't win, so they didn't make plans and believed everything would work out. My mother died in childbirth with me, and Asteria made sure everyone thought I died with her. Instead, I was brought here to the rebellion and brought up as a fighter," she explains to us. "I recently joined the council, and the council sent me to help you escape. There is no one else Nova trusts to ride her, so it had to be me."

"Then why would you call me the true queen of Frayan? Surely that is you," I point out. "I'm an outsider, and you have been here the entire time."

"I'm not a queen, and I never could be. I cannot have children due to an injury," she says, lifting her shirt up to reveal a long cut across her stomach. "The main issue is, I don't have the royal powers. My mother never had a chance to give them to me, and my father never met me before he died after he gave the power to Lilyanne in a last attempt to save his court. I'm a soldier, a council to you in this war, but when it is won, I cannot be the ruler."

"I'm sorry," I say, because I really am.

"Don't be, I've long accepted my fate and my role in the upcoming war. You are the last true royal of Frayan," she tells me, pulling her eyes down to my wrists. She pushes her own sleeves up, revealing bracelets exactly like mine on her wrists. "We tried to fight her once before and terribly failed. To make an example of us, she killed half our people and locked the rest of us up with these. She was so happy about winning the fight that she never really looked at me. I thank the old gods I walked away from her that day, but it means the rebellion has nearly five hundred Fray with no powers."

"I heard most people are losing their magic anyway because of how Frayan is," Jonas states, staring hard at Casella like he is working out a puzzle.

"Frayan is dying, much like it was predicted it would, so yes, the weak will lose their magic. We know the prophecy and the future that is coming for us," she says. "Eventually magic will be nothing but a fairy tale in this world if we don't stop her."

"'How can we trust you? No offence, but everyone in Frayan so far has tried to kill us," Mich says, crossing his arms tightly against his chest. "I don't want Adelaide dead because we trusted a stranger."

"I trust her," I tell Mich, placing my hand on his arm, and he looks down at me. Rick, Nath and Josh look at me as I speak, and this is for them as much as it is for Mich. "I can sense when someone is lying to me; it's an odd power of mine. It only works if I concentrate, and she is telling me the truth. I sense no deception from her."

"All royals have this power. Lilyanne is the only one who does not. The bracelets stop our wings and our other powers, but the ability to sense a lie isn't stopped," Casella says what I've already known.

"Why did Lilyanne not get wings or that power?" I ask.

"Many books and songs speak of how the royal line is blessed by fate. Fate comes to all new royal children and gives them gifts as a blessing. Many believe the fates came to Lilyanne's birth, saw the evil in her eyes and soul, and decided she would receive none of the blessings. Maybe they saw her future and made their choice," Casella says.

"You talk about fates as if they were real people," I reply.

"Many used to call your father a wolf fate," she tells me with a small smile. "A fate linked to the souls of every shifter, every animal on Frayan, and he would only have to call, and they would bow their heads and obey his every word."

"I don't know anything about my father," I say, though I've heard that term before. That voice called me a wolf fate. Maybe it knew my father.

"We have a library here in the academy, though it is a bit messy. The academy is still in ruins, and we can't fix it without attracting too much attention. We mainly use the underground jewel caves to live," she tells us. "Come on, everyone will be waiting to see you all." I remove my hand from Mich's shoulder, only to be surprised when he places his hand on my lower back as we walk after Casella, with everyone following close behind us.

We leave the clearing and head towards a long set of stairs with thin metal gates at the end. They are guarded by two men with blond hair that has streaks of orange in it. Their eyes widen when they see me, and they quickly lower their heads to bow before opening the door.

We walk down the millions of steps that seem never ending before we come out to a big clearing. People are walking around as we emerge, and I look up, my mouth gaping open. The cavern is huge, stretching all the way up like a tunnel, with millions of different types of crystals in the rocks. There are homes in the rocks, balconies made out of the natural stone and covered in little flowers. The sound of laughter and children's giggles comes to me as I stare up at the netted gap at the top of the cavern, which lets natural light reflect off all the crystals. I can see the ruins of the academy above, the towers that are ruined but still tall enough to hide this place. When the sounds of people disappear, I finally look back down to see every single person in the clearing has stopped, and they are on their knees, their heads bowed. I look up again, seeing the balconies are now full of people looking at me in wonder. I don't know what they see. I'm just Adelaide.

"The Autumn court heir has returned. The true queen of Frayan is here to save us all!" Casella shouts, winking at me, and the people burst into cheers that make my cheeks burn red. I don't know how to save them, but I've made my mind up about one thing.

I am going to do everything in my power to try.

I owe my parents that.

I owe Frayan a chance. After all, it's my home.

After I spoke to what seemed like a million people, but in reality it couldn't have been more than fifty, Casella saves me and the guys, explaining that we need to rest after a long day.

"We don't have a lot of suitable rooms, and we usually share the space. I have one room with three single beds, but I thought you could share," Casella suggests with a smile. "It seems your pack would want to keep you close."

"I will need to be near but not *sharing a bed* near," Jonas states. "I'm Adelaide's royal dragon guard."

"And there is a single bed for your guard in the room opposite yours with the other men. Would this work?" Casella asks me, awkwardly ignoring Jonas. He is literally puffing ice fogs from his ears with how annoyed he looks.

"As our pack do not like to be apart, then yes it does work," Rick comments from my side, and Casella looks back at me with a smile. She has all this planned out, like it's clear who should share rooms. I've not even worked any of my relationships out yet. I have no clue if I ever will, but being in a room with all of them is going to be difficult to avoid the subject coming up.

"Casella, we would like a tour of the entire place for safety. I want to know the exit points and all that," Rick asks. "Josh, Mich and Jonas, I imagine you want to come. Adelaide, would you take Nath to rest as his healing sorts out that cut?"

"Of course," I say, and Casella nods in agreement.

"In your room, there will be bandages and natural herb solutions to help such cuts. It's best to wash the cut out with water—the water here has natural healing elements—and then apply the ointment and cover it up," Casella explains to me as we stop outside a wooden door in the hallway. The hallway is lit up with glowing plants in bottles hanging from the ceiling, and it casts a purple glow all around us. There are seven other doors around ours, three on each side and the door at the end which lets you in the corridor. Our room is right at the end of the row, and the door opposite must be where Jonas will be sleeping. It makes me feel better to have him near my pack just in case everything isn't as nice as it seems.

"Thank you for everything," I say, and she nods.

"I will find clothing for you all while we go on the tour. Tomorrow we must have a meeting with the rebellion council," she tells me, placing her hand on my arm for just a second before she walks off. Rick kisses my forehead, not saying anything else, and I meet Josh's eyes for just a second. Before I can warn him it's a bad idea, Josh walks to me and kisses me. Not a little kiss, no, a kiss that can't be mistaken for anything but passionate. I'm helpless to resist him, though I know how tense this is making the situation around us. I can't fight how I feel for Josh.

"Get some rest. We will find dinner for us all, and perhaps we can talk," Josh suggests.

"We definitely need to talk," Rick says as Josh pulls away from me, and I'm sure he smiles at Rick and Mich, who don't look happy. I don't get to see

Nath's reaction as I look back at him, seeing him opening the door and heading inside.

"Many lovers, many problems," I hear Casella say to Jonas, who laughs as he leaves the hallway with her, and my "many lovers" following after them. I nervously rub my hands together as I head into the room, pushing the door closed behind me. The room is pretty simple, three single beds with white sheets and feathery pillows. There is a raised area with wooden walls with a bath in it, a shower much like the one in the cabin we were in, and a toilet. Nath is near the balcony, looking through a woven box on the painted white, wooden cabinet. I take a deep breath, unclipping my cloak and resting it on the bed before heading over to Nath.

"Let me help you. It's my fault you were hurt in the first place," I say, hurrying over.

"Is that the only reason you want to help me, Adie?" he asks, stepping back and letting me take the box. Nath walks to the bed, sitting on the edge as I take out a small bowl and a cloth. I fill the bowl with water from the shower before coming back to Nath, who has taken his shirt off, the cut looking sore and infected.

"It's not the only reason, and you know it," I say as I place the bowl on my lap after sitting on the bed next to him. He faces me as I start wiping the cut, hating how he flinches in pain. He tries to hide it, but he is clearly in a lot of pain. "You're my pack, my family. I hate to see you hurt or in any pain."

"Do you love Josh, Adie?" Nath asks, catching my hand to stop me wiping his cut.

"I love you. I fell for you when we went on our date, when you kissed me, to be exact. I loved you more when you came through the portal to save me, risking everything to come here. I love your cheeky smile, the way you look at me, and how I feel when I'm around you. How you can make me laugh, even when I'm falling apart. Yes, I have feelings for Josh and Rick. I'm not hiding the truth, and I love you enough to let you walk away if that isn't something you can cope with. I will always love you either way." Nath looks utterly shocked, and my heart pounds in my chest as I wait for him to reject me. I don't expect him to be on board with all this, because I've hardly got my head around it all. I was just the girl next door, who they ended up following all the way to another world.

Now I'm asking more of them. "Nath, please say something. Anything."

"I thought—" he stops, shaking his head and moving his hands to cup my cheeks. "I love you. I never expected it to be just me and you. We have a pack, and all of my pack are clearly falling for you. I've never wanted anything as much as I want to spend the rest of my life loving you, Adie." I smile so widely that it hurts my cheeks as Nath leans in to kiss me. His lips press against my own, and I open up to him. When he starts to pull me tightly to him, he flinches from the cut. I clear my throat and swallow, knowing we need to stop.

"Let's sort this cut out, and you need to rest," I tell him, and he softly smiles at me.

"Only if you lie down with me," he asks, and I nod, picking up the rag and getting back to work on cleaning the cut.

No matter how complicated everything is, at least one of my relationships is on the right track.

CHAPTER
SIXTEEN

ADELAIDE

"Sleepyhead, you need to wake up. The meeting is in half an hour," I hear Josh tell me, his fingers tucking some of my hair away from my cheek as I open my eyes. I sit up, seeing that we are alone, and Nath isn't lying next to me anymore. I remember sorting out Nath's injury and then we lay down and clearly slept for a good amount of time. "You slept all night, and Nath didn't want to wake up. They have gone ahead to meet some of the council members. To get a feel for them because the truth is, we don't know who we can trust here."

"I must have been more tired than I thought I was," I say, swallowing a yawn that tries to escape my lips.

"I think it was more a case of you finally being able to rest safely, knowing your pack is here," he tenderly replies to me, his fingers resting on my arm for a single moment before he stands up.

"Sophie isn't here. I can't stop thinking about the fact we can't open the portals, and that means I might not be able to see her again for a long time. I promised a month. That we would only be apart for just one month, and now that is a lie," I say, pushing the sheet back and standing up. I walk to the door to the balcony, pushing it open and looking outside at the deep cavern. The sounds of people talking, children running around laughing, and the general noises from a lot of people fill my ears. This place is so alive and peaceful. It's almost sad that the rest of Frayan isn't like this anymore. I've seen enough of it to know it has changed thanks to Lily's insane ways and how she likes to rule. People can never be free if they fear their queen more than they love her.

"Promises are just words; she knows what's in your heart, and time really doesn't mean anything. Sophie knows we will all come back for her. She is our pack, our family," Josh tells me, meeting my gaze as I try not to feel guilty and let the pain swallow me away. I need to be strong, and part of that is making sure Frayan is a safe place for Sophie to come to. I can't ever keep her or my pack safe while Lily is so determined to kill me. I've made my mind up; I did the moment we were almost hanged for simply existing.

This is my home.

I will avenge my parents and save this world.

"You've decided to save Frayan, haven't you?" he asks.

"You won't hear this often, but you were right, and I was wrong. Frayan is my home, my parents' home, and it needs me. I want to save Frayan; I'm just not sure where to start," I admit.

"The meeting would be a good place," Josh suggests, walking up to me and resting his hands on my upper arms. "You walk in there as the queen they are looking for, and ask for advice on the next move. Let them guide you, and I will make sure they don't control you. No one should do that. You are the rightful heir."

"I'm a girl who was at university hiding a big secret not long ago. Now I've somehow got to figure out how to save everyone," I mutter.

"It's a shame you and Winter didn't spend more time together. You have a lot in common," he chuckles.

"We do?" I ask.

"Winter was brought up as a human, unaware of who she was. She was studying to be a vet when fate found her and demanded so much more. It wasn't always easy, and the price of war broke her heart at times," he explains to me.

"If I start a war and someone dies for me—" I stop because I can't even imagine how to move past that.

"People will die in this war, but you did not start it. Lily did many years ago, and you are going to end it," Josh interrupts me, and I know he is right. I lean up and press my lips to his just briefly, needing the little contact to draw some strength for the next move. I have a meeting to attend.

MY NEW RED cloak sweeps behind me and around the grey dress I'm wearing as I walk into the meeting room, holding my head high as I try not to feel intimidated by the twenty or more people in the room that turn to look at me. All their eyes are fixed on me as Josh shuts the door, and I move over to stand next to Rick, Mich and Nath who are standing in front of chairs. The chairs are laid out in a large circle, and light beams into the room from the large gap in the ceiling that somehow goes outside, so I can see the blue skies above. Jonas moves from the side of the room to stand next to Josh who nods to him briefly. Josh and Jonas stand at my other side in front of their own empty chairs, and everyone else in the room is quick to find a chair to stand behind. I look over at Casella who chooses a chair opposite me and moves around it to stand in the middle of the circle.

"Welcome, Adelaide," Casella says and holds a hand out for me. I meet Josh's eyes as I walk around the chair, and there is so much strength in them. He believes in me, and I must believe in myself. I walk over and stand next to Casella, briefly glancing around at the people in the room as Casella speaks. "This is Adelaide Autumn, the saviour of the prophecy and the rightful heir to the Autumn court. We have all waited many seasons for her return to Frayan, but fate was not ready to bring her here until now. The war finally has two sides. It finally has two queens, and one is on our side. On Frayan's side. We have many plans to make, but Adelaide, would you like to say anything?"

"Y-yes," I stumble on the word and clear my throat, lifting my head high. "My mother was Asteria Autumn, and only a week ago, I met her for the first time, and then I held her as she died in my arms. I knew little of Frayan before I came here, and I will be honest, I did not want to help anyone when I first arrived. I spent my life on the run from this world, and I blamed Frayan for everything that happened in my past. That was until I spoke with Lilyanne and learnt the real truth. *She* is the cause of all the loss and pain, not Frayan. Lilyanne wants the throne that badly that she is willing to burn an entire world down to make sure she gets it. I will not let her do that. I never knew it, but I do now: Frayan is my home. It is where I am meant to be, and if you will have me, I will fight for you. I am here now, and I know who I am."

Casella nods at me before clapping her hands once before crossing her arms on her chest, flattening both her hands and lowering her head. The people in the room one by one do the same thing until it is just me, my pack, and Jonas left watching everyone. Casella lifts her head after a while and places her hand on my shoulder.

"You are our queen, now and until our last breath," Casella explains to me. "Now we will help you win the war. Why don't we all sit down, and I can introduce you to everyone. This first meeting is more to get an understanding of where you are and what you want us to do next."

"I'd like that," I say, smiling at her before we take our seats and I introduce my pack.

"I am interested to learn what armies Lilyanne has and what we have to counter with," Mich asks, resting his hands on his elbows. "The armies are what win a war, and I spent many years learning from kings on Earth about warfare, and I may be able to help. We are all extremely good fighters and good teachers."

"We have an army that is a quarter, if not less, of the size of the army Lilyanne will have, but we train every day, and any help with further training would be a massive help," a man says, drawing everyone's attention to him. He has light red hair, and he is a little older than us, I'm guessing from the wrinkles around his eyes. His cloak is light blue, and as I look around, I start to notice that most of the people's cloaks are blue, except for two who have dark yellow and green cloaks on. "The major reason we can't fight her is because we are all powerless, and her army is not."

"This is Court leader Cirro Winter," Casella explains to me.

"Are most of you from the Winter court?" I ask before anyone can say anything.

"Yes, the Winter court was the second to last court to be attacked in the war. We had started moving our people into hiding when the Spring and Summer courts fell, and we figured out it wouldn't be long until we would be attacked," Cirro answers me.

"There are many Autumn Fray here as well," Casella adds. "Many, if not most, were simply children when they were hidden here to escape the wars." I don't say anything else, sitting back for the next hour as Casella introduces all of the twenty-one people in the room and what they do. Healers, fighters, teachers and everything in between, but I get the feeling this isn't enough to win the war. Not when Lilyanne has an army a lot bigger than the size of our own, and they must have better weapons and armour than us. I rub my wrists where the bracelets are a permanent reminder of how I will never be able to fight against Lily and actually win. She has the advantage while I'm like this, and she will never release the bracelets.

"I believe there isn't much more to be said today. I'd like to show Mich and whoever else wishes the army we have and see if there are any improvements we can make," Cirro states, standing up, but I keep my eyes locked onto Rick's as he stares at me like he can read my mind. "It might be a simple point that we don't have numbers."

"I will stay with Adie," I hear Rick tell the others as we all stand up. I don't wait for any of them as I go to the door and walk straight out, not looking back once as I head down the corridors, passing many people as I pull my hood to try to stop them bowing. I start running up the stairs and down the corridor to our room and head inside. I only stop to sit on the edge of the bed, sucking in a deep breath. I know Rick was following me, a deep part of me could sense that despite how my powers are completely locked away. I don't feel like myself, and I have no clue how to get it back. Rick moves in front of me after shutting the door, and he kneels down, placing his hands over mine.

"No one expects you to have all the answers. No one expects you not to be scared shitless about this war, we all are. I just know we have to win this war and not give up, Adie," Rick tells me, trying to make me feel better.

"I'm not giving up. I'm powerless, and what use is a queen with no power?" I say.

"The fact you are fighting and being strong, even with no powers, is everything. Can't you see that? They love and respect you more because they see you are scared like them, but you are here anyway," Rick replies. "Strength is worth more than power right now."

"I don't want to let them down. I don't want to let *anyone* down, Rick," I admit, because that is what I am truly most scared of.

"The only way you could let them down is by running away. We both know you wouldn't do that; it's not the woman I'm in love with," he delicately tells me.

"Rick...I can't shift. I might never be able to again, and it means—"

"That we can't find out if we are true mates or not, but you know what?" he asks, and I shake my head. He lifts a hand, placing it on my cheek. "I don't care about fate. I know in my soul I'm meant for you." I move a tiny bit closer and kiss Rick like I can never kiss him again. He groans as I deepen the kiss, moving my hands into his hair and feeling how soft it is. He pushes me back onto the bed, never breaking the kiss as he presses his body into mine. A little moan escapes my lips as his body perfectly fits between my legs.

"Wait," I say against his lips as his hand starts to unclip my cloak, and he pulls back to look at me.

"We can take it slower if you—"

"No, I want this. You. I j-just haven't done this before," I admit, nervously biting on my lip.

"Mating?" he asks with a frown, and my cheeks light up. That's not what I meant. "I've never mated to anyone else either, Adie. You can only do that once. Do you not want to be my mate? We can wait—"

"I've never had sex, Rick. That's what I meant," I mumble and sigh when his eyes widen. "And I'd be honoured to be your mate, I'm just nervous about this."

"Are you sure you want this?" Rick asks me.

"Positive. It doesn't put you off that I'm—"

"It doesn't. If anything, I love that I will be your first, and we can always remember this time together," he tells me, and I can tell he means it simply by how he looks at me.

"Kiss me then," I tease as I undo my cloak,

letting it fall around me on the bed, and he smirks at me just before he does as I ask. I pull at his shirt as his lips slowly explore my own, and he leans back, pulling it off for me as he kneels between my legs. I run my fingers over his rippled muscles on his stomach and up to his chest. His breath quickens with every little movement I do, and I find I love to watch him. I think he knows it too. Rick slowly pushes up my long grey dress, which is simple in its design, and I help him tug it off over my head. I try to read his expression as he runs his eyes over my body, which thanks to all my clothes needing a wash, I don't have any underwear on.

"You're perfect, Adie. Beautiful and unforgettable," he says, sliding his hands down my thighs as he leans down over me. I lean up and kiss him, gasping at the pleasure as he presses his body into mine, and his hands cover my breasts. His fingers run across my nipples, and the pleasure quickly builds as Rick swallows the moans escaping my lips. He moves to my side, keeping his eyes locked on mine as he pulls back and slides his hand down my stomach until he finds my core. My back arches as he finds my clit, gently rubbing circles that soon send me crashing into a surprise orgasm. I've had exes do this before, but they never got me here as quickly as Rick just did. When everything comes back to me, I look over to see Rick gazing at me, and I notice something else. His teeth are different than I've ever seen him. I reach up, and he catches my hand.

"I'm sorry, it's been a while since I've had blood. I need to hunt soon," he admits to me.

"Don't be sorry. You need to bite me to mate, right?" I ask, pushing him onto his back and swinging my legs over his hips. His hands tighten on my thighs as he watches me, not stopping me though.

"Yes," he grits out.

"Then take what you need. Nothing about you scares me, Rick. Nothing," I say, and I can see he needed to hear that. The relief in his eyes is almost hard to see. I gasp as he leans up and kisses me, turning us over and pinning me to the bed. I help him undo his trousers, and he kicks them off as I run my hand over his hard, long length. Rick lines himself up, leaving his lips inches away from mine so he can look into my eyes as he slowly slides into me. I cry out in pain as he pushes in, and he whispers into my ear, distracting me from the pain.

"It will fade. I love you," he tells me, keeping still when he is fully inside of me. The pain soon fades away into nothing but pleasure as Rick slowly thrusts in and out of me. As another orgasm starts to build up, Rick kisses me almost softly, and I arch my neck for him.

"I want my mate to make me his," I moan.

"You never have to ask," Rick tells me before kissing my neck gently. The moment he bites me, I cry out in a pure mix of pain and pleasure as an orgasm slams into me. Rick growls, a long growl that makes me shiver as he finishes and lets go of my neck. He looks down at me, my blood on his lips, and I run a finger across his bottom lip. I shiver from the connection I now feel to him, like his emotions are my own, and I can sense them. I feel connected to Rick on a level I can't even explain.

"I love you, Rick," I whisper to him.

"I love you, Adie," he tells me and kisses me once more. I wrap my arms around my mate, forgetting the world for just a little longer.

SEVENTEEN

"Do you love her?" Rick asks me, coming into the training room as I lower the sword I am holding. I rest on the handle as Rick shuts the door and crosses his arms as he waits for my answer.

"Yes," I answer him, and I can see he doesn't exactly love that answer. "Adelaide—"

"Is now my mate," Rick proudly interrupts to tell me. I should have guessed that cocky, loved up smile wasn't for nothing.

"Do you plan to stop me loving her?" I ask him, curious. It almost hurts that he is mated to her now, but then I did expect it to happen at some point. She loves him. Adelaide loves all of my pack, and it's so clear she has since the first time she met them. I don't think I will ever forget the first time I saw her, so strong and perfect as she faced me down. Everyone is usually scared of me in some way, but not Adelaide. Or at least she did a brilliant job of hiding her fear. Her fiery red hair, which is soft and stunning, matches her fiery personality.

"No. That would hurt her because she loves you," Rick says with a sigh, coming over and sitting on the edge of the wooden platform I'm standing on. I walk over and place my sword down before sitting next to him.

"And Nath," I comment.

"And Mich. When did this all get so complicated?" Rick asks, and I shrug.

"I don't know, but in some ways, it gives me hope for our future. We could have what our mum and her mates have," I say to him.

"You're different here," he points out, looking at me. "Something has changed."

"My demon side is almost blocked here, or at least, it doesn't control me as much," I explain to him, and I see the relief in his eyes way before he tries to hide it. I don't blame him. I'm a better person now, and I know it has a lot to do with everything that happened.

"Is that what you want?" he asks me.

"Yes," I admit, looking at him. "I never thanked you for sticking by my side when I was a total tool. I fucked up, more than once, and you never left."

"You're my brother," he says, like that explains everything.

"Same here. I will always have your back," I tell him honestly.

"I should hope so, considering how many times I've had to save your ass," he replies, and we both laugh. He has a point.

"Congratulations on finding your mate, Rick," I tell him.

"Same to you," he comments. "I'm sure it won't be long until you officially mate."

"We have a war to win here. For Adelaide," I point out. From what I've seen of their army and the weapons, it isn't going to be enough to flat out beat Lily. We need a sneaky plan or something else to help us. I wish we could just open a big portal to Earth, because I know Winter would happily send her armies through and help us win this. Right now, we are on our own, and we have to figure this out ourselves.

"She can win this war without us, I know it. I don't think she has a clue how truly amazing she really is," Rick points out, and he is right. I've watched a scared girl somehow turn into a confident woman that is willing to do anything to save the world she was born in. I'm proud of her, much like I know Rick is too.

"We will support her until she does," I reply.

"Where are Nath and Mich?" Rick asks. "I should tell them about me and Adelaide myself."

"Last time I saw them, they were with Jonas and Casella, taking the piss out of Jonas," I say with a chuckle. "And they already know, maybe not about the mating, but that you love each other."

"Jonas has a big crush on that Casella girl, doesn't he?" Rick laughs.

"Shame she seems to dislike him and is shutting down any of his flirting," I point out.

"We should go and give him some tips," Rick suggests with a cheeky smirk.

"Or make it worse," I suggest instead and fist bump Rick before we leave the room. Everything is a little more complicated than we planned, but our pack will work it out.

We always do.

It's what a family does.

EIGHTEEN

"You must come to me, child of fate. I can show you
your powers. I have what you need. Come to me and
save Frayan. It is the only way..."

I freeze as I hear the voice that has haunted me since I came to Frayan, and I've never known where exactly it is coming from. I look around me on the balcony, seeing nothing as Nath sleeps on the bed in the room, and I hear Mich in the shower.

"Who are you?" I ask the air, but nothing replies to me for a long time as I stare out at the cavern, watching the jewels. I don't know what comes over me, but I place my hand on the purple crystal in front of me, and it starts to glow. One by one, all the crystals in the cavern brightly glow before I hear the voice in my head, but it echoes so loudly it hurts.

"I am calling you, Adelaide Autumn. Time is dear, and it will cost you the war if you do not come to my side. I am the truth. I will whisper to you. I am fate. Come to me, heir of the Autumn court. Heir of fate..."

"Adie!" Mich grabs my arms, yanking me away from the crystals, and they all stop glowing as I collapse into his arms. I rub my ears to stop the ringing as Mich holds me to his wet, very naked, chest. I focus on the three scars on his smooth chest, that look like they were a deep scratch, as I calm my breathing down.

"Did you hear that? Who was it?" Nath says, kneeling in front of us and looking sleepy. I hadn't even noticed he was here; I was too confused by everything.

"You heard the voice? The woman?" I ask Nath, who nods.

"I heard it too, in the shower, so I quickly grabbed a towel and ran out to check on you. Adie, you were glowing gold like the sun, and every crystal was so bright it hurt to look at them. I had to pull you away; it didn't look right," he tells me, and I frown, wondering how that even happened.

"It hurt," I admit. "It's never hurt before."

"Before?" Nath asks, frowning at me. "Tell us everything. We need to know to keep you safe."

"Since I've come to Frayan, I've heard the voice talking to me several times. Always asking me to come to them and calling me a wolf fate," I admit to them.

"We should go and get the others. We need advice on this," Mich says and clears his throat. My eyes widen when I realise I'm sitting on his lap, when he is wearing just a towel and in front of Nath as well.

"I need to go to the voice. I feel like it is the right thing to do," I say as I stand up, thankful I have my leather clothes back and my thick cloak on. "It feels urgent that I find her." My cheeks light up when I move a little, feeling that Mich more than likes me sitting on his lap. He doesn't seem as embarrassed as I do though. If anything, he is amused.

"Go ahead. I will quickly grab some clothes," Mich says with a smirk in my direction at how flustered I am. Nath takes my hand, chuckling to himself as we walk into our room and out into the corridor. We bump into Rick and Josh, who are followed by Casella and Jonas.

"We were just coming to check on you. I felt your pain," Rick explains to me, checking me over with his eyes as he comes to my other side. Josh leans against the wall, watching me closely as Casella and Jonas wait nearby.

"I'm okay, but I need to find the woman who spoke. I feel it is important. She has been speaking to me since I came to Frayan," I explain to them.

"It's the voice of fate. We hear her sometimes to guide us when we are lost or in danger. If she calls, you must answer," Casella firmly states.

"Do you know where she is?" I ask.

"Many say your mother loved a fate, a wolf fate to be exact. There was a pack of wolves which lived in the Autumn court before the war, they lived right behind the castle. Maybe there are some of them still alive there, and they may be able to help," Casella suggests.

"She calls me a wolf fate," I whisper, though they all hear.

"We never did know who your father truly was," Casella gently says. "Maybe he was the wolf fate, leader of the wolves of Frayan. I am not sure; I wasn't alive around then, and so many of us here were children when we were hidden so our parents could go and fight the wars. They never came back to tell us the information we needed to know."

"This woman knows though. I must go to her," I say, looking at my pack.

"I can send someone to—"

"It has to be me. I know it's dangerous, but I also know you are an heir of the Winter court. You can lead if anything happens to me," I say, because it's true.

"You are the queen, now and forever, Adelaide," Casella states. "But the other half of you is calling, and the fates are never wrong. I will track a safe path through the woods for you. You can follow the coast line to the Autumn court, and it leads straight to the castle."

"I could fly—"

"Jonas, I want you to stay and keep this place safe. I have four fighters, and I will be okay," I tell him. "Help them get the army ready and protect Casella."

"I am your dragon guard, and I would not feel—"

"Jonas, you are also my friend. Please understand that I have to go with my pack to the Autumn court castle," I tell him. "My past is there, and I need my pack to support me alone in this."

"It's more a ruin than a castle now. Lilyanne destroyed it many years ago," Casella warns me. "It once was one of the most beautiful castles in Frayan. There are drawings in the library I could show you one day."

"Of course she did," I mutter and shake my head. "Jonas, I need you to protect my people, the rebellion, and I'd love to see those drawings one day, Casella."

"It would be smarter to travel in a small pack. That way you have less chance of being seen," Casella says, and we all wait for a moment before Jonas tensely nods.

"Time for a road trip, pack," Rick says, clapping his hands.

"It's not exactly a road trip when there are no roads," Josh points out.

"What are roads?" Casella asks with a frown. I

guess they wouldn't have roads here; from what I've seen, it's all stone or dirt pathways. "Never mind. I have a boat to get ready for you and plans to make."

"We best get to the weapons room and stock up," Rick says and kisses my cheek before heading off with Mich and Josh.

"Want to head to the kitchens? We should pack what we can for the trip," Nath asks.

"Sounds good," I reply, leaning my head on Nath's shoulder as we walk down the corridor after the rest of my pack.

I just hope I'm not leading my pack into a danger we can't get out. Either way, I'm going to find the last of the secrets of Frayan.

NINETEEN

I watch as Adelaide laughs with Casella, though I can't hear what it is that is making her laugh. I eat more of the food on the long stone table in the main part of the cavern. Casella and the council have thrown a going away party of sorts with massive tables of food and music being played in the distance. Casella stands up, clapping her hands a few times, and the music is turned off and the talking stops, making the room silent for her.

"As you all know, Adelaide and her pack are off tomorrow to search for something very important to help us win the war. Unfortunately, Adelaide has never seen air dancing, and I don't know about all of you, but I believe it's something so special to

Frayan, and every Fray should do it at least once. Luckily the three sisters from the Winter court came to us from hiding many years ago, and they are blessed with the talent." The people cheer as she stops talking and takes Adelaide's hand, leading her away. Rick shrugs at me, and we both get up to follow her over.

"I'm staying for the food," Nath says, and Josh only places a hand in the air to say he is doing the same thing. I walk over and stop next to Adelaide's side, and she grins up at me as three women wearing long white dresses go into the middle of the circle of people, the bright moonlight beaming down onto them. A haunting tune starts to play, the song different to my ears, and we all watch as the women start dancing. They move in perfect rhythm in circles, spinning around, their long light blue hair flowing around them. Suddenly they start floating into the air, still moving perfectly with the music around them, and I move my eyes down to watch Adelaide as she enjoys the dancers. Her eyes are wide, full of wonder and so bright as she clearly loves the performance. My hand itches to tuck a loose strand of her long red hair behind her ear to feel how soft and smooth it is. Her skin is so pale, looking like the smooth surface of pearls that I liked to collect as a kid. Not that I could tell her that. She would likely think I'm crazy, and the love triangle she has going is complicated as it is. My wolf disagrees entirely though, just like it has since the first moment we met.

She is our mate.

I know it and feel it deep in my soul, but I don't want to make her life more complicated than it already is, and she might not even feel anything for me.

"You should dance with them, Adelaide! The people would love it!" Casella suggests.

"I don't know, I'm not a dancer," Adelaide says, sounding nervous as everyone looks to her.

"Mich is a brilliant dancer," Rick suggests, patting me hard on the back. "You two should dance together."

"Mich?" Adelaide asks, looking up at me, and the question is spoken so nervously that I couldn't say no if my life depended on it. I smile at her, and hold my hand out. I instantly feel calmer the moment her small hand touches mine, and I lean her out into the middle of the dancers, feeling the air blowing under our feet.

"I have no idea what to do," Adelaide admits.

"Let me lead, Adie," I softly tell her, tugging

her into my arms. I swing her around as she fully lets me guide her, and her eyes widen as our feet lift off the ground, until we are dancing in the air, in the middle of the three women.

"Am I doing it right?" she asks, holding onto me tightly. I tilt my head to the side, staring so deeply into her eyes I'm sure she can read my every thought. I might as well tell her the truth.

"You're beautiful, Adie," I whisper to her. Her cheeks burn red as she smiles widely at me, and I spin us around once more. "I could dance forever with you and never notice the world passing us by."

"Are you trying to steal my heart, Mich?" she asks me with a cheeky smile, and I chuckle. She doesn't have a clue how right she is.

"What if I was?" I ask just as the music stops and our feet land on the ground. I step back and bow my head before turning and walking into the crowd that runs towards their queen.

I don't think Adie will ever know how much I wanted her answer.

TWENTY

"Come back to us safely. We are going to make a distraction in the Spring court so no one is looking your way," Casella tells us as I climb out of the boat last, and Casella stays with Jonas inside it. I stand on the rock and take Josh's hand to pull me up to his ledge.

"It's a five-day trip if we make it through the Summer court with no problems," Rick comments, handing Josh a bag he was carrying.

"The Summer court is nothing but sand and beaches. There is no cover if Lilyanne flies over, so you must quickly make it through the court. At night, make sure not to light any fires," she warns us.

"We will make it quickly through the Summer court. Thank you for everything," I tell Casella, and she smiles at me, the wind whipping her light blue hair into her face and across her eyes.

"It was an honour. I hope to be your advisor and friend for a long time," Casella says, and I've found myself wanting just the same thing. I have a feeling we will be friends for a long time, and Casella will become someone I trust very much.

"Come back to us. We need a queen," Jonas says, bowing his head once at me, and Casella does the same thing as she unties the rope holding the boat to the rocks. I wave goodbye to them as they float away and pull their hoods up, before looking back at my pack. We are quiet as we get off the rocks and jump down onto hot sand below. Even through my boots, I can feel how hot it is.

"Time to shift," Rick says, undoing his shirt as Mich and Nath hand one bag to me and one to Josh so he has two. It becomes slightly uncomfortable as they all start undressing, and I start to wish I could shift. Rick shifts first, transforming into a huge black wolf and shaking out his long fur before stretching. Mich is second to shift into a grey wolf, with the tops of his ears missing and three long scars down the right side of his fur. He is still stunning though. Nath shifts last into a white wolf with streaks of blue down his fur, and his blue eyes seem to glow as he walks over to me. I spread my fingers through his hair on his head, and he rubs his head against my stomach in response. Josh takes all our bags and uses some rope to tie them to Mich's back, and this makes me think they have everything planned out.

"You should ride on Nath. I'm going to take Rick and fly for a bit," Josh says like it is nothing at all to be worried about. I get the feeling they have done this before, and I really haven't.

"Ride?" I nervously say, watching as Josh climbs on Rick's back. Josh is riding my mate, perfectly normal. Wolf riding is normal. Nath leans down for me, and I dig my hands into the thick hair on his neck as I climb on his back, and he stands up. Rick howls before he takes off, running so fast across the beach past the sea. Mich is quick on his heels, jumping over a large rock. I gasp as Nath takes off sprinting down the beach, and the salty sea splashes against my face. We race down the beach, and I laugh, actually loving the feeling of trusting Nath completely to carry me. I grin at Josh as he spreads his black wings out and lets the wind blow him up into the air, and then he flies straight towards me. I get nervous as he gets closer and suddenly grabs me around the waist. He shoots us up into the air, making me scream as I grab him closely and wrap my legs around his waist.

"You're cute when you worry," Josh teases with a grin. "You have wings now, or at least you will have them back soon. You need to know there is nothing to be scared of up here."

"It's not up here that I am scared of. I just don't want to fall," I whine.

"The thing is, falling isn't anything to be scared of when you have someone to catch you," he tells me and kisses me. I scream as we drop down through the clouds, and Josh doesn't spread his wings out to stop us. I close my eyes, trying to remember to breathe when suddenly we stop falling, and we are flying over our pack. Josh lets me drop onto Nath's back when I'm close to him, before flying away again.

My wolves howl loudly, making me shiver from the sound.

I love my pack.

CHAPTER
TWENTY-ONE

ADELAIDE

I watch the flames as they bounce in the fire in front of me, embers spinning off into the air and being blown away by the breeze. I don't know how long I watch the swirling embers before I roll onto my back, seeing the deep red trees we have found. The edge of the Autumn court is all purple trees, and they get darker towards the middle until they become this beautiful shade of red that reflects the moonlight and bright stars. We made it through the Summer court within two days, and we have been working our way through the Autumn court for a day. Riding on the wolves has made everything a lot quicker, and so far, we haven't run into any trouble.

"A penny for your thoughts?" Mich asks, leaves crunching under his boots as he walks over to me. I sit up as he moves to sit at my side, taking a rest from his watch. I eye Rick, Nath and Josh who are fast asleep, their light snores almost sounding like a car engine struggling to light up.

"My dad used to say that," I lightly chuckle, pulling my gaze to Mich. "Your ears in your wolf form, do they hurt?" I know it's random, but I've been thinking about it for a while now.

"No, they are part of me now, though I was a little clumsy when I was younger," he tells me, resting his arms back behind him and looking at me. "I once ran head first into a tree. It knocked me out, and I woke up naked, surrounded by my class- mates and Rick's uncle who came looking for me. The arsehole couldn't stop laughing."

"It sounds like you had a good childhood," I chuckle.

"In parts. Before the war, I was a bastard child with a strange power to speak into people's minds. After the war, I was a powerful witch and wolf hybrid, with a real family for the first time," he explains to me. "The queen and kings of the supernatural race taught me how to be a man and to protect our people. When you have good leaders, it is easy to thrive under their instruction."

"What can you do with your witch side?" I ask.

"I am better with water than any other element, though I have some control of fire to make lights, and I can portal anywhere I've been before. Some witches are powerful enough to go anywhere, but they can only take themselves. I can take more people with me, but not unless I'm familiar with the area. Some witches, like Jonas, can't portal at all, but then his dragon can do insane things with ice which is boosted from his witch powers," he explains to me. "I used to hate the witch side of myself because I know my father must have left my mother pregnant and alone. I don't know either of them, and a name is all I have of my mother."

"You had family, though. A name is more than many get," I point out.

"I know that, but I'm still curious." He shrugs. "Curiosity doesn't get you answers though. It's just something you have to live with."

"Josh offered to show me the past using his angel powers. Maybe he could do the same for you," I suggest.

"He has offered it, but it will only show me

pain," Mich explains to me.

"That's why I said no as well," I admit. "I know whatever I will see will hurt."

"This must be hard for you, going to the place you were born and discovering you're expected to save the world. It's a lot of responsibility and a past that must be hard to accept," he says to me, and he has it right there.

"It's part of who I am, much like being in your pack is the same. We all have reasons for being alive, a meaning to our lives. Mine is just a little more complicated and tasking than most," I say. It's what I have started to think now I know Winter had the same thing, a life thrust upon her that she was not prepared for. Now she is queen, and her people are happy and safe. Mine aren't, and I want to help. I need to help.

"I admire you, Adie," he says, and I reach over, nervously placing my hand on his arm.

"Thank you, but I've done nothing to be admired for," I tell him.

"Yes, you have. Many would have given up by now, faced with what you have, but here you are. Beautiful, brave and inspiring," he softly tells me, and for someone that is such a closed book most the time, he is so open with me right now. I can read all the emotions in his eyes, his expression and body language. It's a little daunting as much as it is seductive.

"I feel like I'm a human facing a supernatural war with no clue what to do," I admit to him.

"You aren't human, and you never have been, but a deeper part of you knows that you were brought up around humans and understand their traits. Being human is something pretty special, I think," he says and moves his hand to lie on mine. "They don't have to worry about complicated things."

"Like?" I ask.

"How I think you are my destined mate, and I have felt it since we met. Nath feels the same, and Rick is already your mate. I see Josh is in love with you...these sorts of things," he gently tells me, even though he is dropping a bombshell on me. Mich has never given me any suggestion he thought I was his mate.

"Mich—"

"We have forever to figure us out if you even want an us. If you don't, I will leave when this war is over. I only want to see you happy," he explains to me.

"And what would make you happy?" I ask.

"Kissing you," he simply tells me, though the simple reply makes my heart beat fast enough it blocks out all other sounds. He moves closer to me, placing his hand on the base of my neck and rubbing his thumb softly along my jawline. I stare into his dark brown eyes that flicker with the reflection of the flames in them as I move closer, almost touching my lips to his. I slide my fingers through his hair, loving the softness. We both don't move a long time, just embracing how close we are, neither of us willing to make the first move to end this.

"I like you, Mich," I eventually whisper, though it sounds like I shouted the words.

"I like you too, Adie," he tells me. "And I'm taking this, no matter how complicated it might turn out to be."

Then he kisses me.

Mich kisses me like I belong to him, all of my heart and soul. He deepens the kiss, exploring every part of me at the same time I figure out what he likes. I find myself sinking deeper into his arms, into this new part of our relationship.

I can't help the one thought in my mind...what happens when everyone finds out how deeply in love I am with each of them?

TWENTY-TWO

"**W**elcome to the Autumn court," I say, reading the old wooden sign we have found, and I can see the ruins in the far distance in a field of red flowers that grow around the broken building, flowers the same colour as my Fray bracelet from my father.

"I can't read that, it's just symbols. How can you?" Josh asks from my side as Rick, Mich and Nath shift back and get dressed.

"I don't know, I just can," I say, shrugging my shoulder.

"It's Frayan text, which I can read too. Anyone with Frayan blood can," Nath says, clearly overhearing our conversation as he comes out of the woods, tying his belt up.

"It's an old sign, looks burnt in places anyway," I say, walking to it and placing my hand on the edge. No more stalling, I have to find the truth out one way or another. I'd rather find out all the answers to my past, and whatever that may bring, before I go into a war with Lilyanne, not having a clue how to win. Maybe there are some answers here that could help with the war?

"It's going to be okay, whatever we find here," Rick gently says.

"What if there is nothing left?" I ask.

"Then you have us," Josh answers, nodding to me once. Josh is completely right; I have them, and that is enough no matter what I find in these ruins. The woman that has been calling to me might not even be here in the first place.

Rick slides his hand into mine as we start walking down the pathway, with Mich and Nath keeping behind us. Josh stays a little ahead, and all of us are completely on guard as we get closer to the ruins. It's almost heartbreaking to see what is left of a massive castle turned into nothing but broken white pillars covered in vines and weeds. The vines have the same red flowers on them as on the ground, covering and winding their way through all the broken stone. They look like my tattoo, and they match the colour of my bracelet too. We keep walking down the pathway, past the line of fallen pillars, until we get to the castle remains. I'm sure once the castle towered into the sky and was stunning to see, but now it's nothing more than a pile of stone, cracked and broken. Just like my past with Frayan. How am I meant to find any answers in nothing but broken stone?

"You did not come here for answers to your mother's history. You came to find out your father's, Adelaide," a kind, soft-spoken woman states as she walks out from behind the castle. She has long white hair that almost glows on its own and blue eyes so clear it's hard to keep looking at them. She is wearing a long white dress, which makes her seem almost otherworldly.

"Rick!" Tay shouts in pure joy, beaming from the shoulder of the woman she is sitting on. She flies straight to Rick, wrapping her little arms around his neck and hugging him closely. Her eyes find me as Josh speaks.

"If you are even thinking of hurting Adelaide—"

"I would never hurt my family," the woman is

quick to correct him, making me pause all the same. Her bright blue eyes meet mine as I look her over, searching for anything that would make us look related and finding nothing but a sense of familiarity.

"How are we related then?" I ask her, crossing my arms, and her eyes track the movement before meeting my gaze again. She seems to focus on my father's bracelet for a long moment, and I wonder if she recognises it. I spot a similar one on her wrist, though the stones are blue.

"I am your aunt, a wolf fate omega, and the last of my kind. My brother was the last wolf fate alpha, and you carry his blood. I see the same strength from you as I did from him," she says. "You are the saviour."

"What was my father's name?" I ask, feeling a tear fall down my cheek. Shock and excitement fill me as I stare at my aunt. I have family left here on Frayan.

"Axis. And he loved you before you were even born. I never got to see you as a baby, and I couldn't hide you here. My brother gave me all his power and forced me to leave with his pack, hiding us from the world until the time you came home," she tells me, walking closer, and I take a step closer to her. Rick tugs my hand, and I shake my head at him.

"I trust her," I tell him, I tell them all as they watch.

"And we trust you," Nath says, placing his hand on Rick's shoulder as Rick lets me go.

"What is your name?" I gently ask.

"Lazuli, and I am so happy to finally meet you," she says, offering me a hand. "It's time you became who you are meant to be, Adelaide Autumn."

"What is that?" I ask, slowly moving my hand to hers. The moment my hand touches hers, a bright gold light beams out of our hands like a gush of wind.

"A wolf fate. Alpha to all wolves. This is your fate," she tells me as she places her other hand over mine, the gold light still beaming out. Lily's bracelets on my wrists snap open and fall to the ground like they are nothing, as the gold light travels up my arms. "I bless you with the power of fate. May you rule true and always protect the path of light, Adelaide Autumn."

"What is happening?" I ask with a gasp, feeling more power and energy than I ever have before. It makes me fall to my knees, and she falls with me.

"It is my time to leave the worlds. I cannot be with you in your struggle, but the wolves of Frayan will always come for your call. So will every animal in Frayan...w-we h-have waited for the t-true queen to return." With every word she says, a part of her fades away until there's nothing.

"Don't—" I pause as a scream leaves my lips, and Lazuli fades away into nothing but gold light that blasts into the sky as I fall to my side. I look up to see gold dust fall around us and back down to my hands which are covered in gold flowered tattoos that shine brightly. The bracelet glows, and I feel like my father is with me for just a second. My mother too.

"Adelaide?" I hear my pack calling for me, but I know there is another pack that will heed my call. I stand up, my movements and the words that leave my lips feeling like someone else is directing them. I raise my arms high into the air and throw my head back, closing my eyes.

"I am the wolf fate. I call my pack; I call the wolves of Frayan. Come to your alpha." I shift as the last word leaves my lips, and I feel the power of my call blasting out around me.

"Adelaide, look," Josh says, his voice nothing but wonder as he flies in the air to my side. I slowly turn around, seeing Nath, Rick and Mich all in wolf form, their heads bowed down, but behind them, hundreds of wolves line the pathway and the surrounding trees. They are a rainbow of colours, and every single one of them is also bowing. Gold dust floats around them and us, almost like the fates themselves are blessing us.

I lift my head and howl, my howl echoed as my packs join in.

Thanks to the past and to my family, we might have a chance of winning the war.

Queen Lilyanne will not be the queen of Frayan for long.

The crown is mine.

EPILOGUE

The cold wind of the Winter court blows around my cloak, pushing it to the side of me as I stare at the frozen ice lake in front of me. Something has changed, I can feel it. The magic of Frayan seems somewhat...hopeful. I do not wish Frayan to hope. Adelaide will not save them; she cares for something else much more than she does Frayan.

Or to be exact, *someone else.*

My spy somehow managed to send a magical letter through to this world, which appeared in front of me somewhat randomly. Witch magic, I suspect. If my spy can contact me, it means the Earth queen can contact Adelaide and the others. It is not what I wish to hear.

199

A portal burns up on the ice, and a girl is thrown through it, her passed out body sliding across the ice until she stops at my feet. Her brown hair sticks to the ice below her, and blood trickles from the cut on the side of her head. I wait a few seconds, and a second portal appears with my soldier jumping out of it to land a little away. I hear the shouts of a man on the other side of the portal, but it's too late for the Earth queen and her kings to do anything as it slams shut.

Queen Winter is clearly as stupid as the rest of her family was. Fates are nothing to be scared of, just silly fairy tales. Adelaide's father died simply, so all fates can be killed just as easily no doubt.

"My queen, I did as you planned. This girl was important to Adelaide. I listened and observed for ten years, and the stones I used are the last way to get here. No one will follow us," the man states, though I've forgotten his name and what I promised him for spying for me. I'm sure he had a family he wanted to save, though I believe I killed them already.

"Good. That is excellent to hear," I say.

"My family? Will you free—" He screams, a weak cry really, as I slam a beam of sunlight through his chest, leaving a hole. He falls to the ice, and I look back to my prize as she starts to wake up.

I lean down as she looks up and starts to scream before shifting into a tiny brown wolf. The moment she tries to run away, I click my fingers, and two guards run, grabbing her easily off the ice and bringing her back to me as she tries to bite their fingers off. I grab her muzzle, tightening my hand around it until she starts to cry, and I just laugh.

"Sophie, welcome to Frayan. I believe your sister was missing you."

ABOUT G. BAILEY

G. Bailey is a USA Today and international bestselling author of books that are filled with everything from dragons to pirates. Plus, fantasy worlds and breath-taking adventures.

G. Bailey is from the very rainy U.K. where she lives with her husband, two children, three cheeky dogs and one cat who rules them all.

(You can find exclusive teasers, random giveaways and sneak peeks of new books on the way in Bailey's Pack on Facebook or on TIKTOK— gbaileybooks)

FIND MORE BOOKS BY G. BAILEY ON AMAZON...

LINK HERE.

PART ONE
BONUS READ OF
HER WOLVES

DESCRIPTION

I knew nothing about mates until the alpha rejected me...

Growing up in one of the biggest packs in the world, I have my life planned out for me from the second I turn eighteen and find my true mate in the moon ceremony.

Finding your true mate gives you the power to share the shifter energy they have, given to the males of the pack by the moon goddess herself. The power to shift into a wolf.

But for the first time in the history of our pack, the new alpha is mated with a nobody. A foster kid living in the pack's orphanage with no ancestors or power to claim.

Me.

After being brutally rejected by my alpha mate, publicly humiliated and thrown away into the sea, the dark wolves of the Fall Mountain Pack find me. They save me. The four alphas. The ones the world fears because of the darkness they live in.

In their world? Being rejected is the only way to join their pack. The only way their lost and forbidden god gives them the power to shift without a mate.

I spent my life worshipping the moon goddess, when it turns out my life always belonged to another...

This is a full-length reverse harem romance novel full of sexy alpha males, steamy scenes, a strong heroine and a lot of sarcasm. Intended for 17+ readers. This is a trilogy.

CHAPTER
ONE

)) ● ((

"Don't hide from us, little pup. Don't you want to play with the wolves?"

Beta Valeriu's voice rings out around me as I duck under the staircase of the empty house, dodging a few cobwebs that get trapped in my long blonde hair. Breathlessly, I sink to the floor and wrap my arms around my legs, trying not to breathe in the thick scent of damp and dust. Closing my eyes, I pray to the moon goddess that they will get bored with chasing me, but I know better. No goddess is going to save my ass tonight. Not when I'm being hunted by literal wolves.

I made a mistake. A big mistake. I went to a party in the pack, like all my other classmates at the beta's house, to celebrate the end of our schooling and, personally for me, turning eighteen. For some tiny reason, I thought I could be normal for one night. Be like them.

And not just one of the foster kids the pack keeps alive because of the laws put in place by a goddess no one has seen in hundreds of years. I should have known the betas in training would get drunk and decide chasing me for another one of their "fun" beatings would be a good way to prove themselves.

Wiping the blood from my bottom lip where one of them caught me in the forest with his fist, I stare at my blood-tipped fingers in a beam of moonlight shining through the broken panelled wall behind me.

I don't know why I think anyone is going to save me. I'm nothing to them, the pack, or to the moon goddess I pray to every night like everyone in this pack does.

The moon goddess hasn't saved me from shit.

Heavy footsteps echo closer, changing from crunching leaves to hitting concrete floor, and I know they are in the house now. A rat runs past my leg, and I nearly scream as I jolt backwards into a loose metal panel that vibrates, the metal smacking against another piece and revealing my location to the wolves hunting me.

Crap.

My hands shake as I climb to my feet and slowly step out into the middle of the room as Beta Valeriu comes in with his two sidekicks, who stumble to his side. I glance around the room, seeing the staircase is broken and there is an enormous gap on the second floor. It looks burnt out from a fire, but there is no other exit. I'm well and truly in trouble now. They stop in an intimidating line, all three of them muscular and jacked up enough to knock a car over. Their black hair is all the same shade, likely because they are all cousins, I'm sure, and they have deeply tanned skin that doesn't match how pale my skin is. Considering I'm a foster kid, I could have at least gotten the same looks as them, but oh no, the moon goddess gave me bright blonde hair that never stops growing fast and freckly pale skin to stand out. I look like the moon comparing itself to the beauty of the sun with everyone in my pack.

Beta Valeriu takes a long sip of his drink, his eyes flashing green, his wolf making it clear he likes the hunt. Valeriu is the newest beta, taking over from his father, who recently retired at two hundred years of age and gave the role to his son willingly. But Valeriu is a dick. Simple as. He might be good-looking, like most of the five betas are, but each one of them lacks a certain amount of brain cells. The thing is, wolves don't need to be smart to be betas, they just need the right blood-line and to kill when the alpha clicks his fingers.

All wolves like to hunt and kill. And damn, I'm always the hunted in this pack.

"You know better than to run from us, little Mairin. Little Mary the lamb who runs from the wolf," he sing songs the last part, taking a slow step forward, his shoe grating across the dirt under his feet. Always the height jokes with this tool. He might be over six foot, and sure, my five foot three height isn't intimidating, but has no one heard the phrase *small but deadly*?

Even if I'm not even a little deadly. "Who invited you to my party?"

"The entire class in our pack was invited," I bite out.

He laughs, the crisp sound echoing around me like a wave of frost. "We both know you might be in this pack, but that's only because of the law about killing female children. Otherwise, our alpha would have ripped you apart a long time ago."

Yeah, I know the law. The law that states female children cannot be killed because of the lack of female wolves born into the pack. There is roughly one female to five wolves in the pack, and it's been that way for a long time for who knows what reason. So, when they found me in the forest at twelve, with no memories and nearly dead, they had to take me in and save my life.

A life, they have reminded me daily, has only been given to me because of that law. The law doesn't stop the alpha from treating me like crap under his shoe or beating me close to death for shits and giggles. Only me, though. The other foster kid I live with is male, so he doesn't get the "special" attention I do. Thankfully.

"We both know you can't kill me or beat me bad enough to attract attention without the alpha here. So why don't you just walk away and find some poor dumbass girl to keep you busy at the party?" I blurt out, tired of all this. Tired of never saying what I want to these idiots and fearing the alpha all the time. A bitter laugh escapes Valeriu's mouth as his eyes fully glow this time. So do his friends', as I realise I just crossed a line with my smart-ass mouth.

My foster carer always said my mouth would get me into trouble.

Seems he is right once again.

A threatening growl explodes from Beta Valeriu's chest, making all the hairs on my arms stand up as I take a step back just as he shifts. I've seen it a million times, but it's always amazing and terrifying at the same time. Shifter energy, pure dark forest green magic, explodes around his body as he changes shape. The only sound in the room is his clicking bones and my heavy, panicked breathing as I search for a way out of here once again, even though I know it's pointless.

I've just wound up a wolf. A beta wolf, one of the most powerful in our pack.

Great job, Irin. Way to stay alive.

The shifter magic disappears, leaving a big white wolf in the space where Valeriu was. The wolf towers over me, like most of them do, and its head is huge enough to eat me with one bite. Just as he steps forward to jump, and I brace myself for something painful, a shadow of a man jumps down from the broken slats above me, landing with a thump. Dressed in a white cloak over jeans and a shirt, my foster carer completely blocks me from Valeriu's view, and I sigh in relief.

"I suggest you leave before I teach you what an experienced, albeit retired, beta wolf can do to a young pup like yourself. Trust me, it will hurt, and our alpha will look the other way."

The threat hangs in the air, spoken with an authority that Valeriu could never dream of having in his voice at eighteen years old. The room goes silent, filled with thick tension for a long time before I hear the wolf running off, followed by two pairs of footsteps moving quickly. My badass foster carer slowly turns around, lowering his hood and brushing his long grey hair back from his face. Smothered in wrinkles, Mike is ancient, and to this day, I have no clue why he offered to work with the foster kids of the pack. His blue eyes remind me of the pale sea I saw once when I was twelve. He always dresses like a Jedi from the human movies, in long cloaks and swords clipped to his hips that look like lightsabres as they glow with magic, and he tells me this is his personal style.

His name is even more human than most of the pack names that get regularly overused. My name, which is the only thing I know about my past thanks to a note in my hand, is as uncommon as it gets. According to an old book on names, it means Their Rebellion, which makes no sense. Mike is apparently a normal human name, and from the little interaction I've had with humans through their technology, his name couldn't be more common.

"You are extremely lucky my back was playing up and I went for a walk, Irin," he sternly comments, and I sigh.

"I'm sorry," I reply, knowing there isn't much else I can say at this point. "The mating ceremony is tomorrow, and I wanted one night of being normal. I shouldn't have snuck out of the foster house."

"No, you should not have when your freedom is so close," he counters and reaches up, gently pinching my chin with his fingers and turning my head to the side. "Your lip is cut, and there is considerable bruising to your cheek. Do you like being beaten by those pups?"

"No, of course not," I say, tugging my face away, still tasting my blood in my mouth. "I wanted to be normal! Why is that so much to ask?"

"Normal is for humans and not shifters. It is

why they gave us the United Kingdom and Ireland and then made walls around the islands to stop us from getting out. They want normal, and we need nothing more than what is here: our pack," he begins, telling me what I already know. They agreed three hundred years ago we would take this part of earth as our own, and the humans had the rest. No one wanted interbreeding, and this was the best way to keep peace. So the United Kingdom's lands were separated into four packs. One in England, one in Wales, one in Scotland and one in Ireland. Now there are just two packs, thanks to the shifter wars: the Ravensword Pack that is my home, who worship the moon goddess, and then the Fall Mountain Pack, who owns Ireland, a pack we are always at war with. Whoever they worship, it isn't our goddess, and everything I know about them suggests they are brutal. Unfeeling. Cruel.

Which is exactly why I've never tried to leave my pack to go there. It might be shit here, but at least it's kind of safe and I have a future. Of sorts.

"Do you think it will be better for me when I find my mate tomorrow?" I question...not that I want a mate who will control me with his shifter energy. But it means I will shift into a wolf, like every female can when they are mated, and I've always wanted that.

Plus, a tiny part of me wants to know who the moon goddess herself has chosen for me. The other half of my soul. My true mate. Someone who won't see me as the foster kid who has no family, and will just want me.

Mike looks down at me, and something unreadable crosses his eyes. He turns away and starts walking out of the abandoned house, and I jog to catch up with him. Snowflakes drop into my blonde hair as we head through the forest, back to the foster home, the place I will finally leave one way or another tomorrow. I pull my leather jacket around my chest, over my brown T-shirt for warmth. My torn and worn out jeans are soaked with snow after a few minutes of walking, the snow becoming thicker with every minute. Mike is silent as we walk past the rocks that mark the small pathway until we get to the top of the hill that overlooks the main pack city of Ravensword.

Towering buildings line the River Thames that flows through the middle of the city. The bright lights make it look like a reflection of the stars in the sky, and the sight is beautiful. It might be a messed up place, but I can't help but admire it. I remember the first time I saw the city from here, a few days after I was found and healed. I remember thinking I had woken up from hell to see heaven, but soon I learnt heaven was too nice of a word for this place. The night is silent up here, missing the usual noise of the people in the city, and I silently stare down wondering why we have stopped.

"What do you see when you look at the city, Irin?"

I blow out a long breath. "Somewhere I need to escape."

I don't see his disappointment, but I easily feel it.

"I see my home, a place with darkness in its corners but so much light. I see a place even a foster wolf with no family or ancestors to call on can find happiness tomorrow," he responds. "Stop looking at the stars for your escape, Irin, because tomorrow you will find your home in the city you are trying so hard to see nothing but darkness in."

He carries on walking, and I follow behind him, trying to do what he has asked, but within seconds my eyes drift up to the stars once again.

Because Mike is right, I am always looking for my way to escape, and I always will. I wasn't born in this pack, and I came from outside the walls that have been up for hundreds of years. That's the only explanation for how they found me in a forest with nothing more than a small glass bottle in my hand and a note with my name on it. No one knows how that is possible, least of all me, but somehow I'm going to figure it out. I have to.

CHAPTER
TWO

)) ● ((

"Wake up. You have a book on your face."

Blinking my eyes open, I see nothing but blurry lines until I lift the book I was reading off my face and rub my nose. Damn, I must have fallen asleep reading again. I close the human-written romance book about demons at an academy and turn my gaze to where my foster brother is holding the door open. Jesper Perdita has dark brown, overgrown hair that falls around his face and shoulders, and his clothes are all a little too big for him and torn in places because they are hand-me-downs. But he smiles every single damn day, and for that alone, I love him. At just eight, he acts the same age as me thanks to losing his family a year ago and having no relatives offer to take him in. I don't care that we aren't blood-related, somehow I'm always going to be here for him, because he hasn't had a childhood any more than I have. We are foster kids in a pack that hates our very existence, and they make damn sure we know about it.

The fact they keep him alive is just because one day he might have a powerful wolf when he turns sixteen. If he doesn't, he won't have any family to save him from what happens next. I'm a little luckier in the sense I will find a mate, every female always does at the mating ceremony in the year they turn eighteen, and my mate will have no choice but to keep me alive. Even if he hates who I am, our fate is linked from the second the bond is shown.

"What time is it, Scrubs?" I ask, needing to pull my thoughts from the ceremony to anything else before I freak out. He twitches his nose at my nickname. That came from how many times he needed to scrub his face of dirt and mud every single day. He is the messiest kid I've ever seen, and it's awesome. I want a different future for him, one where he could have the same last name as everyone in the pack other than the foster kids. We are given the last name Perdita, which means *lost* in Latin, because we are lost in every sense of the word.

Everyone else in the pack shares the same last name as the pack alpha. Ravensword.

"Six in the morning. We have to leave for the ceremony in an hour, and Mike said you need to bathe and wear the dress in the bathroom," he answers. He looks down, nervously kicking his foot. "Mike said something about brushing your hair so it doesn't look like a bat's nest."

I snort and run my hand through my blonde hair. Sure...I might not have brushed it a lot, but the unruly waves don't want to be tamed.

"I won't go, get a mate and never come back. You know that, right?" I ask him, sliding myself out of my warm bed and into the much colder room. Snowflakes line my bedroom window that is slightly cracked open, and I walk over, pushing it shut before looking back at Jesper. He meets my gaze with his bright blue eyes, but he says nothing.

"Whoever finds out you're their mate is going to want you to start fresh. Without this place and me following you around. I might be eight, but I'm not stupid," he replies. Floorboards creak under my feet as I walk over to him and pull him in for a hug, resting my head on top of his. The truth is, I can't promise him much. The males in mating have control over the females, and to resist that control is painful, so I'm told. That's why the moon goddess is the only one who can choose a mate for us, because if it went wrong, it would be a disaster for all involved.

"If my mate does, then I will figure out a way to get him to let me see you. The moon goddess will not give me a mate I am going to hate. All mates love each other," I tell him what I've heard.

"I don't like goodbyes," he replies, pulling away from me. "So I won't come with you today. I won't."

"I get it, kid," I say as he walks to the stairs. He never looks back, and I'm proud of him, even if it hurts to watch him make another choice that only adults should have to make. I head back into my small bedroom, which has a single bed with white sheets and a squeaky mattress, and one chest of drawers. I grab my towels and head down the stairs to the only bathroom in the old, very quirky house. The bathroom is through the first door in the corridor, and I shut the door behind me, not bothering to switch the light on as it is bright enough in here from the light pouring through the thin windows at the top of the room. Peeling dolphin-covered wallpaper lines every wall, and the porcelain clawfoot bathtub is right in the middle of the room. A cream toilet and a row of worn white cabinets line the other side, with a sink in the middle of them. Hanging on the back of the door is the dress I have dreaded to see and yet wanted to because it's the nicest thing I am likely ever going to wear.

The mating dress is a custom-made dress for every woman in the pack, paid for by the alpha to celebrate the joy-filled day, and each is made to worship the moon goddess herself. Mine is no different. My dress is pure silk and softer than I could have imagined as I run my fingers over it. The hem of the dress is lined with sparkling white crystals, and the top part of the dress is tight around the chest and stomach. The bottom half falls like a ballgown, heavier than the top and filled with dozens of silk layers that shimmer as I move them.

As I stare at the dress, the urge to run away fills me. The urge to run to the sea and swim to the wall to see if there is any way to get out. Any way to escape the choices I have been given in life.

Mike was right, I can't see the light in the pack, because the darkness smothers too much. It takes too much.

I step away until the back of my legs hit the cold bathtub, and I sink down to the floor, wrapping my arms around my legs and resting my head on top of my knees.

One way or another, the mating ceremony is going to change everything for me.

"Do hurry, Irin. We have a four-hour drive, and this is not a day you should be late like every other day of your life!" Mike shouts through the door, banging on it twice.

"On it!" I shout back, crawling to my feet and pushing all thoughts of trying to escape to the back of my mind. It was a stupid idea, anyway. The pack lands are heavily guarded, and they would scent me a mile off. After a quick bath to wipe the dirt off me and wash my hair, I brush my wavy hair until it falls to my waist in bouncy locks, even when I know the wind will whip them up into a storm as soon as I'm outside. The dress is easy to slip on, and I wipe the mirror of the steam to look at myself after pulling my boots on.

My green eyes, the colour of moss mixed with specks of silver, look brighter this morning against my pale skin, framed by blonde, almost golden, hair. I look as terrified as I feel about today, but this is what the moon goddess wants, and she is our ancestor. The first wolf to howl at the moon and receive the power to shift.

She will not let me down today.

I nod at myself, like a total loser, and walk out of the bathroom to find Mike and my other foster brother waiting for me. Mike huffs and walks away, mumbling something about a lamb to the slaughter under his breath, and I look at Daniel instead. His brown eyes are wide as he looks at me from head to toe, likely realising for the first time the best friend he has is actually a girl. He is used to me in jeans or baggy clothes, following him through the muddy forest and not giving a crap if every single one of my nails is broken by the end.

And I never wear dresses. Not like this. Daniel runs his hand through his muddy-brown hair that needs a cut before he smiles.

"Shit, you look different, Irin," he comments with a thick voice. Daniel is one year older than me, and when he was tested for his power last year, he was found to be an extremely powerful wolf. He is next in line to be a beta if anyone dies, which would be a big thing for a foster kid to be a beta. Either way, he is free of this place, and who knows, he might even be my mate. A small part of me hopes so because Daniel is my best friend, and it would be so easy to spend my life with him. I don't know about romance, as I have never seen him like that. He is good-looking in a rugged way, so I guess we could figure it out.

"Nervous about today?" I ask him, as this is his second mating ceremony, and it's likely he might find a mate. It's usually the second or third ceremony where males find their mates, but for females, it's always the first.

He clears his throat and meets my eyes. "Yeah, but who wouldn't be?"

"Me. I'm totally cool with it," I sarcastically reply. He laughs and walks over, pulling me into a tight hug like he always does. This time, I hear his wolf rumble in his chest, the vibrations shaking down my arms.

"If you're mated to a tool, I'll help you kill him and hide the body. Got it?" he tells me, and I laugh at his joke until he leans back, placing his hands on my shoulder. He moves one of his hands and tips my chin up so I'm looking at him. "I'm not joking, Irin. I don't care who it is, they aren't fucking around with you."

"Mates are always a perfect match," I reply, twitching my nose. "Why would you think—"

He lowers his voice as he cuts me off. "You don't live in the city like I do, and I can tell you now, mates are not a perfect match. Not even close. The moon goddess...well, I don't know what she is doing, but you need to be cautious. Very cautious because of your background."

"Why didn't you tell me this before?" I demand.

He shrugs. "Guess I didn't want you to over-think it and try to run. I can't save you from what they'd do if you ran, but I can protect you from a shitty mate. I.e., threaten to break every bone in his body if he hurts you."

"Daniel—" I'm cut off as Mike comes back into the corridor and clears his throat.

"Get in the car, now. It looks bad on me when we are late!" he huffs, holding the front door open. Daniel uses his charming smile to make Mike's lips twitch in laughter as I hurry to the front door and step out into the freezing cold snow. It sinks into my dress and shoes, but I welcome the icy stillness to the air, forcing me to stop over worrying for a second.

"Always daydreaming, this one," Mike mutters

as he passes me, talking to Daniel at his side. "Her eyes are going to get stuck looking up in the clouds one day."

"At least I'd be seeing a pretty view for the rest of my life," I call after Mike as I hurry after them down the path to the old car waiting by the road. We don't use cars often, only today and travelling to funerals is permitted, mostly because the cars are old junk that make a lot of noise and take up fuel. Daniel pulls the yellow rusty door to the car open, and I slide inside to the opposite seat before doing up my seatbelt as Daniel and Mike get in the car. Mike drives and Daniel sits next to me rather than shotgun.

About ten minutes into the drive, I realise why Daniel sits next to me as my hands shake and he covers my hand with his.

Please, moon goddess, choose Daniel or someone decent. I don't want to become a mate murderer in my first year as a wolf.

CHAPTER
THREE

)) ● ((

Flickering, multicoloured lights drift across my eyes as I wake up, finding my head lying on Daniel's broad shoulder, his arm wrapped around my waist, and it's so unexpected, I jolt up, almost hitting my head against Daniel's chin. He moves super fast, with reflexes his wolf gives him, and just misses my head. I slide out of Daniel's arm, and he clears his throat, straightening up on his seat and running a hand through his thick hair. Rather than talk about that awkward moment, I turn and look out the window, frost stuck to its edges, to see we are driving down by a cliff that overlooks the glittering sea between Wales and Ireland. I've been to this place once when I was fifteen on a school trip

233

to see where a mating ceremony is held and what we should expect for our future.

If anywhere in this world made me believe in magic, it was this place. A place that has been in my dreams for so many years. For most wolves, this is the place they will meet their wolves and start their new life. For me, it's a way of escaping my past and finally finding out what the moon goddess wants for me. It can't be this life I have, the torture at the hands of pack leaders, the pain of being an outcast with no family.

I catch Mike's eyes in the middle mirror and see a little sadness in them like always, because he has heard and seen all the horrors the pack has forced on me throughout the years. Protecting me was something he has struggled to do, because, at the end of the day, he couldn't be everywhere.

"Nearly here, aren't we?" Daniel interrupts my thoughts, and I'm thankful for it. That's a dark memory lane to go down. "They should let you wear a coat over the dress, it's freezing."

"I've never cared about the cold," I remind him, gazing back out of the window as we pull up in the gravelled area by the cliff. Several groups of people are standing around or walking down the stone cliff pathway to the beach that is marked with fire lanterns on wooden poles every few metres, making the walk look eerie and frightening.

"You can do this, Irin. You've been brave ever since you were found in the woods, half-starved, dirty and alone. Look at you now," Mike tells me as he turns the car off, meeting my line of sight through the mirror. "You are a woman this pack will be honoured to have. Now hold your head high, put the past away and show them. Show them who you are, Irin."

My cheeks feel red and hot as I wipe a few tears away and force my hands to stop shaking as I grab the handle of the door. I can't tell him, not without my voice catching, that I will miss Mike and his words of wisdom. His kindness and general attitude towards life, the ways he has shown me how to be strong even at my lowest points. Pulling the door handle open, I step out onto the lightly snow-covered ground, and the cold, brittle sea air slams into me, making me shiver from head to toe. I can taste the salt in the air and smell the water of the sea and hear it crashing against the sand below us. The wind whips my hair around my face as Daniel walks past me, looking back once before he walks down the path to join the other men at the beach where they have to stand. Mike moves to my side, and we simply wait as all the men leave for the path down to the beach, while the women, us, wait at the top for our time to descend.

Some parents linger for a while before they walk to the edge of the cliff in the distance where there's a massive crowd of spectators waiting to watch the magic of the mating ceremony. Mike leaves eventually to join them, never glancing back at me. The girls all gather, pretending I don't exist like they always have done since I turned up at their school. A small, tiny part of me hurts that not a single one of the forty-two girls in my class who have known me six years even looks my way.

I'm invisible to them, to my pack, to everyone.

Rubbing my chest, I gulp when the bell rings. A single, beautiful bell ring fills the air to start the beginning of the mating ceremony, and tension rings through the air as everyone goes silent. Like ducks in a row, the women all line up, and of course I move right to the back, behind Lacey Ravensword, someone who has never even looked my way, even though she is considered a low potential mate because of her father trying to run away from the pack, and he was killed when she was a toddler. Even she, with her family basically betrayers to the alpha himself, is higher ranked than I am. She flicks her dark brown hair over her shoulder, glancing back at me and sneering once with her beautiful face before turning away.

The cold seeps into my bones by the time the line moves enough for me to walk, and my legs feel stiff with every step, the nerves making me feel so close to passing out right here and now. Every single step off the cliff and down the path feels torturous until I see the beach.

Then everything fades into nothing but pure magic. In the centre of the sandy yellow beach is a massive archway, sculpted into two wolves with their noses touching where they meet in the middle. The wolves are so high the tips of their ears touch the heavy clouds above us, and icicles line the grooves of the fur on their snow-tipped backs. In the centre of the archway, one of the first females steps into the pool of water under the archway, sinking all the way under completely before rising and swimming slowly through the archway. The water suddenly glows green, lit up with magic from the moon goddess herself.

The young lady with long black hair climbs out of the pool on the other side, her entire body glowing green with magic, and the magic slowly slips from her skin, turning itself into a swirling ball of energy and shooting away from her. It flies into the crowd of wolf shifter men waiting on the other side, all of them too hard to really see from here, and there are cheers when the mate or mates are no doubt found. I can't see who the female goes to as the cliff winds around, but I hope she is happy with her new mates. Daniel's warnings about mates not always being happy fills my mind, making me more nervous than ever before, because what if he is right? What if I end up with a mate who I hate and he hates me?

I trip on a small rock, slamming down onto the path and hissing as my hand is cut. I look up as Lacey turns back, and then she just laughs, leaving me on my knees on the path as she carries on behind the queue. Tears fill my eyes that I refuse to let fall, and I stand up, seeing my dress is now dirty with sand and mud, and I lift my hand to see blood dripping down my palm to my wrist from a long cut. Sighing, I close my palm and let my blood drop against the wet sand as I know I have to carry on down this path.

What feels like forever later, I get to the beach and look across to see Lacey waiting behind three other classmates, just as one of them steps into the water. Four left before my fate is decided. I'm tempted to slip my shoes off, to enjoy the feel of the cold sand under my bare feet, but I keep my boots on. I don't want to lose them. I walk over the beach, feeling so many eyes watching and judging me. I refuse to look at the men on the other side, knowing the new alpha will be there, and seeing him brings up so many dark memories. He was just the alpha's son back then, back when we were fifteen and he tricked me by pretending to be my friend.

Now he is the alpha, at only eighteen, after he ripped his father to pieces four months ago. The pack is scared of him, but me?

He terrifies me.

Keeping my eyes down, I only look up to see Lacey step into the water with perfect poise and elegance I could never master in my wildest dreams. She sinks under the water, and it glows bright green, and this close, I can feel the magic like it's pulling me towards it. The water is enchanting, and I can't take my eyes off it until the glow fades, and I glance up to see the magic surrounding Lacey as she stands on the other side of the pool. The magic leaves her body and gathers in a ball, before slamming left and straight into the chest of one of the men near the front.

Not just any man.

Daniel.

He stands in pure shock, looking at the green magic bouncing around his skin before he looks up at Lacey, and then he turns to me. Our eyes meet, and silently I try to tell him it's okay.

Even when it feels like a storm has just started in my chest and that storm is going to take every bit of hope from me.

Daniel doesn't move for a long time, and Lacey follows his gaze back to me, her eyes narrowing as I quickly look away and back to the water. Out of the corner of my eye, I see Lacey walk to Daniel, and he places his hand on her back, leading her away from the crowd and towards the pathway to the crowds of people waiting at the top of the cliff to celebrate with them. To cheer about their mating.

And now it's my turn.

Everything is silent, even the violent sea and snow-filled sky seem to still for this moment as I take a step forward and my foot sinks into the warm water. It instantly glows green, so bright it hurts my eyes, and pulls me in, my body almost betraying my fear-filled mind as I sink into the water until my head falls under. The green light becomes blinding as I float in the water, seeing nothing but light, until a voice fills my mind.

"You are my chosen, Irin. My chosen."

Something appears in my hand as I'm pushed up to the surface, and I gasp as I rise out of the water on the other side, almost stumbling to my feet on the sand, seeing the green magic swirling around my body in thick waves. It bounces, almost violently, in swirls and waves before pulling away from me into a giant ball of green magic, much bigger than anyone else's.

Why the hell do I have to stand out in this of all things? With so many people watching? I can't bear to look or hear anyone as I watch the sphere of magic spin in the air before shooting across the sand right into the man in the middle of the pack.

A man of my nightmares.

A man who took my innocence, crushed it, and made me fear him.

The alpha of my pack.

CHAPTER
FOUR

)) ● ((

The silence is damning. Damning and hollow as I stare into the unfeeling hazel eyes of the wolf shifter who is apparently my fated mate. An alpha doesn't share his mate, so this is the only man in the entire world who the moon goddess believes I should be with. And he is a monster. The alpha doesn't move as green magic crackles around his body, picking up his fur cloak that hangs off his large shoulders. Thick black hair falls to his shoulders in a straight line, not a strand out of place, and his stern face is stoic as he looks at me. Water drips down my dress, my wet hair sticking to my shoulders, and all the warmth from the water is gone now. The magic is gone, replaced only with fear for what happens next.

"No."

His single word rings out across the beach to me, the few yards that are between us are like nothing. No. No to the mating? No, it being me the moon goddess chose as the alpha's mate?

I agree with him...hell no. Mating with this excuse of an alpha, a man with no soul and a scar on his chin I caused when I was fifteen, is a life I would rather not live. Only once have I ever thought about giving up on my life, once on a wintry day like this, caused by the same man I'm looking at right now. This is the second time I have wanted to give up completely.

Whispers and gasps from the crowd of wolves behind him and from the crowds on the cliff finally reach my ears, and I try to block out what they are saying even when some of their words are perfectly heard.

"Her? The alpha's mate? Disgusting!"

"Maybe the moon goddess made a terrible mistake."

"He should kill her and be done with it."

The whispers never stop, and the same thing is

chanted as the alpha's eyes bleed from hazel to green, his wolf taking over. Then he takes one step forward towards me, and I itch to run, to turn and leave as fast as I can, but something tells me not to.

Maybe that bit of stubborn pride I have left. Mike always said pride is a bigger killer than any man. I can see his point as my legs refuse to move and I stay still as a deer caught in a wolf's gaze. The alpha walks right up to me, his closeness making me feel sick to my stomach as he grabs my throat and lifts me slightly off the ground. Not enough to strangle me or cut my airways off, but enough to make me gasp, to make me want to struggle. I claw at his arm to get him off, but I'm nothing but a fly buzzing around a cake to him. I can see it in his eyes, his eyes owned by his wolf.

"How did you trick the moon goddess herself into believing a rat like you could ever be an alpha's mate?" he demands, and when I don't answer, he shakes me harshly, tightening his grip for a second. A second enough for me to scream and gasp, coughing on air when he loosens his grip. He shakes his head, his eyes bleeding from green back to hazel. To think I once trusted those hazel eyes, I dreamt about them, I thought he was my real friend.

"I asked you a question, Irin."

"My name is Mairin to you, not Irin. M-my friends call me Irin, Alpha Sylvester Ravensword. Kill me if you're going to do it. I have feared you for so long that you killing me is nothing more than the goddess giving me my wish."

The lie falls from my tongue easily, even if his name does not. The moon goddess never gave me my real wish, my wish I begged her for once, to kill him, the alpha's son, Sylvester Ravensword. Instead, in some twisted version of fate, she made him alpha and me his mate he has waited for. His eyes stay hazel, but in the corners I see the green struggling to take over. He slowly tightens his grip around my neck, and I close my eyes, wanting to see nothing in these last moments. I gasp as I struggle to breathe, instinctively smacking and scratching at his one hand holding me up by the neck. Fear and panic take over, making my eyes pop open just as I'm thrown across the sand. With a slam, I hit the hard sand on my side, and a cracking noise in my arm is followed by incredible pain as I scream.

"Irin!" I hear Daniel shout in the distance, a wolfy and deep noise just before a foot slams into my stomach once. Then twice, then again and again. The pain almost becomes numb when my voice gives out, and the kicks finally stop as I roll onto my back, looking up at Alpha Sylvester as he angrily kicks me one more time before stepping back, rubbing his hands over his face repeatedly.

"No one follows us. If anyone does, I will rip them to shreds," I hear Alpha Sylvester demand, and the noise of wolves fighting nearby mixes with the sound of the waves. A hand digs into my hair and pulls me up as I taste blood in my mouth. Everything is blurry as someone drags me by my hair and arm over sharp rocks that cut into my back and catch on my dress, but part of me detaches from my body, drifting into a world of no pain as I fade in and out of consciousness. Eventually I'm dropped onto grass, and I blink my eyes a few times, coughing on the blood in my mouth and turning my head to the side, every inch of my body hurting so badly the pain threatens to knock me out with every breath. A hand wraps around my throat once more, and I'm lifted into the air, my feet hanging as I struggle to breathe.

"Open your eyes," Alpha Sylvester demands, his fiery breath blowing across my face.

Opening my eyes is harder than I thought it

would be, and when I do, I see he is right in front of me.

"I can't kill you, because my wolf will not allow it." He shakes me once. "Die in the sea for your fated mate, Irin. Die like you should have so many years ago, because if the sea does not take you, I will know. I will know, and I will never stop sending wolves to kill you. I have rejected you as my mate, you are not worthy of me, and you never could be. You are nothing."

"Then why does the moon goddess think otherwise?" I whisper back with all the strength I have. I should plead for my life, I should beg and cry, but I just stare at him as his eyes flash with pure anger, and he roars as he lets me go. The wind cannot catch my body as I fly off the cliff, well aware the sea is going to take my life in seconds.

And in those seconds I fall, I still pray to the moon goddess for someone to catch me.

CHAPTER
FIVE

)) ● ((

"Get the healer ready!" a deep voice demands, nothing more than a groggy sound to my sore ears as I struggle to wake up. Coldness like I've never known controls my body from head to toe, and it's not just cold, I'm soaking wet too. Every inch of my body hurts. Even my eyelids ache as I pull them open to see rocks in front of me. Smooth white rocks. Waves crash in the distance, and I can smell nothing but damp water. Lifting my head, which takes more strength than I thought it would, I see I'm still in my mating ceremony dress, but it's ripped around my stomach, and a large cut snakes down my ribs, hidden under the ripped fabric of my dress. My bare feet are stuck in the wet sand, and I'm curled up in a space between a group of rocks like the sea threw me here.

Flashes of memories attack me quickly. The sea. The mating ceremony. The alpha who was meant to be my mate but instead tried to kill me... How am I alive?

Scuffling of heavy booted feet reminds me I'm not alone, and I jump away from the noise behind me, pivoting to see a man standing on the rock. His silhouette blocks out the light, making all around him glow as I drift my eyes up his body. Thick black trousers cover large thighs, and he has a black shirt tucked into them. The shirt stretches across his large shoulders, large enough to make him a champ at a rugby match if he chose it. Following my eyes up over his golden skin, I suck in a deep breath when I see his face.

He is beautiful in a way men shouldn't be allowed to be. Strong jawline, high cheekbones, perfectly shaped lips and thick black eyelashes that surround clear blue eyes that remind me of a lake—still, in an eerie way that makes you wonder if there is any life below the waters. Black locks of hair that are a little too long, falling just over his eyes when the wind blows, look softer than the silk dress I'm wearing.

No one in my pack ever looked like him. I would have noticed.

The more I stare, the longer I realise he is staring right back at me, like he has seen a ghost. Like I'm familiar to him. Considering where I came from, he might have done. Not that I have a clue where we are. I lean up on my one arm, but I can't see out of the rocks or anything around the man standing over me.

Correction: the wolf. He is watching me like a wolf, that I am certain of. He is too direct, too inhuman like, and all that I need to see now is his eyes glow.

"Do you know me?" I ask, my voice throaty, and I clear it, tasting nothing but thick salt left over from the sea.

The man tilts his head to the side. "Why are you here?"

"I-I was..." I pause because I have no idea where I am, and telling this wolf I'm the alpha's rejected mate might not be the best idea if I'm still in Ravensword lands. He will drag me back to the alpha, who will try to kill me again. No, I can't do that.

"Answer me."

The man's command is clear, ringing with

power and frustration. I look up, meeting his eyes once more even when I can't think straight or of a single word to say. Whatever I say is going to get me killed, and I can't help but think I've been given a second chance at life. I should never have survived falling into the sea, not with the injuries I have, not when I passed out, but here I am. Alive.

It's clear the moon goddess has much more planned for me than I know.

When I don't say a word for a long time, he moves. The man moves so quickly, and within seconds he is in my face, leaning over me on the rocks. His nose gently touches mine, my body a mix with fear and curiosity.

"Tell me," he commands once more. "Tell me why you are on the shores of the Fall Mountain Pack, or you will die this very second."

Fall Mountain Pack?

Oh my god... How am I alive and on this island? I know people usually die who try to swim between the islands, but for me to have gotten here unconscious is nothing short of magic. I'm yet to decide what kind of magic, considering all I know about the Fall Mountain Pack is that they are cruel and vicious. That they live in ways most wolves would never do or even think about. They don't trade with the Ravensword Pack, and every attempt at peace has been met with death. We are told they are monsters, and now I'm on their lands.

But truthfully, I'm dead either way. If they send me back, the alpha will kill me, and if I stay here, it's likely they will kill me.

I have nothing to lose by telling this man the truth.

"My name is Mairin Perdita, and I am a rejected mate of the Ravensword Pack," I announce, leaning back against the rocks and curling my legs underneath myself, needing space from his man. His eyes widen, but he doesn't say a word. "The mating ceremony named me as the alpha's mate, and because I am a foster child with no family or worth, he rejected me. After hurting me in anger, he tried to kill me by throwing me off a cliff. How I'm here, alive, is a mystery to me, but I guess I am asking for your help. I'm asking for a damn miracle, because my life has been anything but one."

"I would wager surviving your rejection is a miracle. The sea is a cruel mistress at the best of times, and last night was one of the worst storms seen in years," he finally replies, leaning back, his voice less hostile than it was. "I can always tell when someone is lying to me, and you are not, Mairin Perdita. My name is Alpha Henderson Fall, and I am going to help you."

"You're the alpha?" I whisper in shock and a little fear. It shouldn't surprise me he is so high in rank, just because of how commanding and powerful he comes across as, but it does.

"One of the four," he answers and moves closer. "You are weak, my wolf senses it, and I must carry you. Will you allow me? It is a twenty-minute walk to the lighthouse where there is a healer."

The part of me that hates being touched, especially by men, makes me want to say no and stubbornly try to climb out of these rocks myself. But I know I can't. Every inch of me hurts, my stomach is bleeding, and my ankle looks swollen. Somehow I have survived the sea, but without help, I will not survive much longer. I nod once, unable to actually agree, and I'm sure my hesitancy shines in my eyes as he comes closer and wraps his arms underneath me before effortlessly picking me up. In order to steady myself, my hands go out around his neck, brushing against a necklace there that is tucked into his shirt. Henderson jumps out of the rocks, and I look around me to see a tall mountain right in front of us, and a small forest lies between the beach and the mountain. The mountain is topped with snow, and several caves look like they have lights inside from this distance. The beach is long with rocky sand and harsh waves that crash against everything they hit, and in the distance, I see a faded blue lighthouse with its bright light turning in circles. Henderson is silent as he jumps off the rocks into the sand and eats up the space between us and the lighthouse with his enormous steps. After a few minutes, I relax my shoulders a little.

"Is it just luck you found me, or do you live around here?" I question.

Henderson looks down at me, his blue eyes hard to read. "What do you know of my pack, Mairin?"

"That you are monsters," I tell him, remembering well how he said he could sense if I was lying.

His lips tilt up into a dazzling smile. "Lies are so easily told to those who live in fear, and your alpha lied, Mairin. We were never the monsters, but our life differs greatly from where you have come from. Here we don't have fated mates, we only mate with who we fall in love with. Wolves are free to date, to explore, to do whatever they want, and the only new wolves we accept into the pack are rejected or lost. We respect loyalty, and we take in those who are nothing to others."

"There have been other rejected mates?" I ask.

His smile falls. "I collect over one wolf a week from this shore. All of them rejected and thrown into the sea because their mate could not convince their wolf to kill them."

"I had no idea," I whisper.

"To answer your question," Henderson states, shifting me a little in his arms, "I do not live here, but I am called to the lighthouse every day to check out who has arrived. If you had lied to me, or if you were someone who just escaped the pack, then I am tasked with ending your life. We do not take in those who desert their pack and family. We want only those who will be loyal."

My heart beats fast in my chest, hearing the sincerity of his voice. He would have killed me. "So you kill for loyalty?"

"No, I kill for my pack," he answers, his tone clarifying that is the last of our conversation, and I rest back, watching the sea and the very outline of the land in the distance, hidden by clouds. All I can think of is Daniel and Jesper, and even Mike. I have to hope they look after each other, because I can't ever go back.

The Ravensword alpha is my mate, and he will do worse than reject me next time, he will have someone kill me.

So I have to make the Fall Mountain Pack my new home, whatever it takes.